Vivian
Divine
Is
Dead

LAUREN SABEL

Vivian Divine is Dead

KATHERINE TEGEN BOOKS
An Imprint of HarperCollins Publishers

Katherine Tegen Books is an imprint of HarperCollins Publishers.

Vivian Divine Is Dead
Copyright © 2014 by Lauren Sabel

Library of Congress Control Number: 2014933031
ISBN 978-0-06-223195-6

Typography by Joel Tippie
14 15 16 17 18 LP/RRDH 10 9 8 7 6 5 4 3 2 1
❖
First Edition

To my husband, my sword, and my family, my shield

Chapter One

My name is Vivian Divine. I have a secret. I know how I'm going to die.

No one would believe me if I told them. Not that I would. Or could. Someone's always watching. Sometimes I see the tip of a gray head in my window, or an eye behind a fish tank. They're always there: a silver sedan pulling out of my driveway, a glimmer of gold in a dark room.

My dad says he doesn't see anything. I know he doesn't. He doesn't see me.

Since my mother died six months ago, he's lost himself in his work. Now the only time I see him is behind a camera. He's the most famous director in Hollywood, and that means he's busy all the time—too busy for me. But he still finds time to go to all the right parties, make all the right appearances. Last month, he skipped my sixteenth birthday party to go to *another* honorary memorial for Mom. We're talking caviar and champagne, everyone forgetting to be sad in their designer dresses. When he got home, I said, "You missed my birthday again." I almost added, *like the last five years*, but I stopped myself.

"I was working," he said, as if he's ever not working. At least, in the Before, he had a reason to come home, a reason he cared about. Now he's out every night, drunk on his own misery.

In my life, there's always a Before and an After. In the Before, when I was an Oscar nominee for best actress, as one of the youngest stars in history, Mom and I wore matching heart necklaces to the ceremony. In the After, when I was voted Etv!'s Teen Actor of the Year, my mom was dead and my heart was broken.

I don't remember much about the morning my mom was kidnapped, but I do remember that she wasn't wearing makeup. For a woman who'd been voted Hollywood's most beautiful woman three years running by *Celebrity* magazine, that's a big deal. She didn't even go to bed without putting on lipstick first. But that day, she dropped her lipstick and didn't pick it up. We all forgot about it. Dark red melted into the carpet by my room.

Three days later, when the police found her facedown, a knife through her back, an *Etv! Memorial Special* was broadcast on her life—and every gruesome detail of her death. I saw it only once, but Dad watched it over and over, whiskey glass in one hand, gun in the other.

So when I found a DVD of Mom's *Etv! Memorial Special* in my fan mail this morning, I couldn't bring myself to watch it, but I saw the note. It wasn't typed on a typewriter, or in cutout newspaper letters, like you see in movies. It was just Times New Roman font, like a business letter. It said:

This is how you die.

Dad wouldn't believe me if I told him. He thinks I'm imagining all of it: the glimmer of gold, the silver sedan, the eye that is sometimes blue, sometimes brown. But Dad doesn't notice anything anymore, especially me. Ever since his suicide attempt was splashed across the news, he's stayed as far away from me as possible. He doesn't want to remember the way I found him, blood winding down his neck from where the bullet nicked him as he pulled the gun away from his head, just in time; how the news said he'd *attempted* to commit suicide, like it was the only thing he'd ever failed at. Dad doesn't like to fail, and since he can't "fix" me, I haven't told him about the nightmares that wake me up screaming, or about the memories I've had of Mom since she died. They always come when I least expect them, and leave me quivering in terror, obsessed with the guilty feeling that somehow, it must have been my fault.

Mary's the only one who knows about my guilt. Since Dad hired her two years ago, Mary and I have been together seven days a week, twenty-four hours a day. We're so close, we finish each other's sentences; we practically breathe at the same time. And she's not only my bodyguard; she's the closest thing I have to a mother now that Mom's gone. Mary knows things about me that no one else does, like the way I haven't felt happy since Mom died, or the ice that's frozen inside of me that keeps getting thicker, separating me from the rest of the world.

The ice I'm afraid will crack and tear me apart.

Mary says it's important to continue working to keep my mind busy. "You'll *r*emember when you're *r*eady," she says, rolling her *r*'s in a thick Latin purr. "Don't dwell on it."

I don't have time to dwell anyway: I always have to be on guard. At home, the paparazzi climb over the fence and pop up in my windows, trying to get shots of me to sell to the papers. At work, I have to watch every step. Sets are dangerous places, according to Mary, and at Star Studios, there are whole sets built to blow up small buildings, light fires, reenact a flood. Some mornings I'm running from wild mechanical beasts, or dodging a hurricane.

You don't want to be in the wrong place at the wrong time, Mom used to say, refusing to let me go out with my boyfriend Pierre another Saturday night. Mary used to tell Mom she should let me be a normal teenager. But Mom said I wasn't a teenager; I was a teen star.

A teen star has a list of rules a mile long: Don't drink. Don't do drugs. Don't curse. Don't get caught on camera without makeup. Don't leave the house without a body-guard. Don't cry in public. I've followed all these rules except one. And Mom was right: tears smear mascara, even the waterproof kind.

Before Mom died, she was always trying to protect me by reading my future in her tarot cards' inky depths. But she's not around to tell me what I need to know now, like why someone would want to kill her, or why I'd get a death threat in my fan mail. Or even why, when the police found Mom's dead body six months ago, she wasn't wearing her trademark earrings, the ones she was wearing the morning she was kidnapped. The ones Etv! called "the jewels in Hollywood's crown" when they were being nice, and "the four-million-dollar mistake" when they weren't. Two five-carat pink diamonds, carved into the shape of roses.

When I get back to my room, Mom's *Etv! Memorial Special* DVD in my hand, Mary is already screaming into the phone. "I don't want Vivian near that scaffolding," she's yelling, her black hair popping out of the tight bun on top of her head.

After two years of being together day and night, I know Mary's expressions like I know my own. When she wakes me up from a nightmare, there are three lines etched into her forehead, freakishly parallel; when she's nervous that the news cameras are too close, her right eye twitches at two-second intervals; and when Mary's scared for my safety, or is tightening the security on my set, a blue vein pulses in her left temple. Since directors don't like changes, and Mary doesn't like to see me get hurt, the two clash, badly and often. "Or I'm pulling her off set," Mary threatens into the phone, her lips pursed under her large brown eyes.

Mary's right to be worried. Last month, when I ditched work to be with my boyfriend Pierre, my body double stepped in for me. That afternoon, while rehearsing one of my scenes, the girl was almost killed when the scaffolding crumpled beneath her.

Of course, it's not unheard of for people to die on set. A helicopter decapitates an oblivious extra, blanks get replaced with real bullets, a harness rope breaks and an actor plunges to her death. But when an actor who looks identical to you ends up in the hospital, it's terrifying. And a little voice in your head keeps repeating: *That should have been me.*

"And I don't want that boy near her," Mary continues,

her voice hoarse from yelling. "After what he did last night . . ."

Last night. Shame and hurt wash over me again, making my head ache and tears spring to my eyes. Pierre, the only boy I've ever loved, and ever will, was caught on national TV kissing my best friend. Mary says I need to move on, how there are "lots of fish in the sea" or something, but I don't think I can. *If he doesn't want me, why would anyone else?*

Not that I blame him for liking my best friend better. Sparrow is gorgeous. She's got this crazy mane of red hair and she's so skinny I can practically wrap two hands around her waist, unlike me. I have plain, curly brown hair, and what Mom used to call *curves.* As if baby fat *curves.*

Mary slams the phone down and turns to me, the vein slowly fading back into her temple. "You okay, honey?"

Am I okay? How do I answer that? My mom was stabbed to death, my dad tried to kill himself, my body double was almost crushed by scaffolding, and my only love cheated on me. And I got a death threat for breakfast. So how am I? *Shitty.*

"Okay," I lie.

Mary cracks all the knuckles on her right hand, our symbol for *Just say the word, and I'll kill him.* It makes me feel a little better.

"Your dad's looking for you," she says. "Want me to call him?"

I shake my head and hand her Mom's *Etv! Memorial*

Special DVD I found in my fan mail. "Just check this out," I say. "I'll find Dad."

I don't have to look hard; If Dad's not at work, there's only one place he'll be. Every night, I see Dad's shadow crawling the hallways, looking for something. I don't know what. But I see where he ends up:

Mom's dressing room.

Dad goes into Mom's dressing room every night now. Sometimes I hear his phone ring, sometimes he talks in hushed tones, sometimes the door's locked when I turn the handle.

Mom's dressing room used to be my sanctuary, the place where my future was built, because she never left the house without reading my tarot cards first. *The Empress*, she'd say, turning over a willowy, blond beauty that I always thought looked like her. I look more like the Holy Fool: with my square cheekbones, pouty lips, and curly brown hair, I always look startled, like I'm about to fall off a cliff. I usually feel that way too.

But Mom saw more in me than I did. She always said I was stronger than I knew, and she always believed in me, no matter what the reviews said or which of my flaws were pointed out by the press. Dad called her "new age" because she believed in things he didn't, magical things, like the wisdom of the tarot and zodiac signs and yoga. She used to wake me up by whispering, "The universe is smiling on you today," and with her around, it seemed true.

Now I'll never hear that whisper again. It's been replaced by the caustic beeping of my alarm clock, and a huge, crushing feeling of emptiness. I can't even look at the cards anymore, because Mom was supposed to teach me the tarot. She was supposed to teach me a lot of things.

Now I feel a drop in my stomach every time I turn the locked handle on her dressing room door at home, the one with the sparkly *P* on it. *P for Pearl, the biggest movie star in decades. My dead mom.* But Dad must have forgotten to lock the door today, because when I turn the handle, it opens. I step into her dressing room, and a shiver prickles up my neck.

Dad's kept everything *identical* since Mom died: the framed movie poster of *Medusa's Revenge*, her first starring role, tilted at an angle on her closet door; the crystals strung across the four corners of the room; her tarot cards spread over her dressing table.

Empress, she called me, *the creature of light.* I shuffle through the deck, glancing at every gold-encrusted card, but I can't find the Empress. *Where is she?*

I open each of the drawers in Mom's dressing table, but no Empress. I shuffle through the cards again, and then I open her jewelry case. Her emerald collection is still lined up from dark to light, and the diamonds of her necklaces glow like secrets in the plush black velvet. It's exactly like she left it. That's why, before I shut the jewelry box, I'm surprised to find something I thought I would never see again:

A pale pink rose, cut from a single pink diamond.

I hate when I don't remember something about my mom. Anything. Every card in her tarot deck. Her favorite crystal. The famous heart-shaped mole above her lips. But an earring she was wearing the day she disappeared? Impossible.

So as soon as I get to the studio, I go to Dad's shoot on the main soundstage. He never misses work, so I know I'll find him there. Dad's proud of the fact that he's only missed one day of work in forty years, from his child actor days to his rise to renowned director, but it just makes him seem old to me. Not that his gray mustache isn't a giveaway that he's *fifty*, over ten years older than my mom was when she died.

Dad's got his back to me, but I can picture perfectly what he's wearing: an angel T-shirt and cowboy boots, his gray ponytail hanging down his back. He thinks it makes him look cool, but it totally doesn't. Especially since he wears the same clothes *every day*. But Dad can get away with it; he's got what Hollywood calls "the touch": everything he touches turns to money.

As usual, Dad doesn't even notice I'm there, so I scoot up next to him, feeling completely invisible. I should be used to it by now, but every time he ignores me it still hurts, like being stabbed with a dagger.

"Where did you find this?" I ask him, pushing my open hand under his nose. He doesn't move from behind the camera.

"I'm shooting, Vivian," he says. Dad's always shooting. He insists on authenticity in every shot, so it takes forever to get each scene right. When I'm working with him, I learn how to break my way out of handcuffs and shoot real BB guns so the viewer hears the lightbulb *pop* when it goes out.

I stomp my feet. "But where did you find it?"

Irritated, Dad looks at the pink rose earring in my open palm. Something freezes; like a piece of film skipping a beat. "Can we talk about this later?" he asks.

I shake my head. "Now."

Dad sighs and looks at me. As usual, it's not going to be a long conversation: he doesn't even bother to turn the camera off. "The police found it," he says, "near where she was . . . you know."

A hard knot swells up in my throat, and I can barely scrape the words out. "Why now?"

"It was caught between the floorboards. A janitor found it when he was mopping." Dad squashes his hair down over a balding spot behind his left ear. "The police kept it for a month, as evidence."

"Evidence of what?"

"I don't know," he snaps, and then softens. "Maybe DNA or something . . . I don't know why it took them so long to find it, but, well, they finally gave it back."

"Where's the other one?"

Dad shakes his head, and his bottom lip trembles slightly. "They never found it." He runs his hand through his hair, and I see a few bald spots peppered into his scalp.

"Are you pulling again?" I ask.

Dad doesn't answer; he just mats his hair down to hide the bald spots. Dad has something called trichotillomania. Mary says it happens sometimes when people go through a stressful situation. They pull clumps of their hair out: it comes out easily, like the hair has also lost the will to live.

"Give it to me," Dad says, so I extend my open hand, the pink diamond sparkling under the studio lights. Dad takes the earring out of my hand and slips it into his pocket.

"What are you gonna do with it?" I ask.

Dad glances at the red blinking light on the camera. "I've gotta get back to work," he says, and turns away from me. Again.

Chapter Two

DAD'S SHOOTING ONE SOUNDSTAGE over from me, so it's not a far run to my set on the studio's back lot. The set for my movie, *The Story of Don Juan*, is pretty elaborate. There's a full plastic graveyard, half a block wide, and cranes are hunched over the three tallest tombs, where Don Juan is eventually pulled to heaven by his dead fiancée, Ines. Suspension cables crowd the air ten feet above the tombs, rigging up to one main point: my flying harness.

At the north edge of the graveyard, Pierre is already here. He's leaning against a plastic tombstone, his cropped white-blond bangs poking out from under his Don Juan hat, talking to the press. I can tell he's enjoying the attention.

Like me, Pierre's been in show business all his life. He knows all the industry's ins and outs: the way to lose a quick ten pounds, how to show your best side for the cameras, how to stay up all night without getting bags under your eyes. And above all, he knows that there's no such thing as bad press. *Even if you cheat on your girlfriend with her best friend.*

Luckily, Mary's by my side, which makes me feel better. I don't think anyone's even noticed her. Her uniform— a slim black suit—is perfect for slipping into my shadow unless I need her. She's so good at it, sometimes I even forget she's there.

Before Pierre notices me, I spin on my heel and stalk over to the director. He holds out my harness, his thick bifocals making him look like an ancient turtle.

"You okay?" he asks.

I'm tired of people asking me if I'm okay. Of course I'm not. I want to ask, *Why doesn't Pierre love me anymore?* I remember how, when I saw him kissing Sparrow on TV last night, I replayed it over and over, my nails cutting into my palms. When my cell phone rang an hour later, I turned it off and went to bed without our usual two-hour "mushy phone chat," as Mary calls it.

But now I just nod and step into my stiff harness.

This scene, where I pull Don Juan to heaven to save him from his sins, is killing me. First of all, Pierre is the actor playing Don Juan, and second, I have to look him in the eyes the whole time, with the sick-puppy-dog look of true love. *That look was so easy before, when I thought we had true love.*

As the grips raise my harness into the air, I try not to think about the day Pierre and I first fell in love. It was a year ago, when we were wrapping up *Zombie Killer*, my blockbuster about an orphan who saves the human race.

Pierre was already a big star, having been the lead singer of Anime, a boy band from Europe. At the wrap party, after he performed his hit single "Sexy Angel," girls surrounded him, all oohing and aahing, but he walked straight past them like they didn't exist, stopped in front of me, and said: *I wrote that song for you.*

A song for me.

Nobody had ever written a song for me. I don't remember what the words were, something about angels and love at first sight. But for the first time in my life, I felt like I belonged somewhere. With *somebody.*

Pierre understood me in ways nobody else had. He knew what it was like to get bad-mouthed for wearing something out of style or staying in bed for a week after a negative review. He knew what it was like to have a father more dedicated to his career than to you, and to feel lucky to get an online "Happy Birthday!" chat on your special day. We were instantly inseparable.

The newspapers called us "the most promising young

couple in Hollywood," and Star Studios signed us for two major films together. There were even rumors going around that he was going to ask me to marry him when I turned eighteen. Rumors I thought were true.

But Mom never trusted him. She didn't like the way Pierre taught me the secret of a good crash diet to lose weight, or how I never saw Sparrow anymore, unless she hung out with both of us, or how radically different our zodiac signs were. That bothered her the most, I think. Pierre was fire and I was earth. *Fires can ravage the earth*, she said. *Be careful.* But none of Mom's tarot cards could tell me about love, so I didn't listen.

At Mom's funeral, Pierre sang a song he wrote for her. For days afterward, he held me, stroked my unwashed hair, and kissed my lips with a force that made me forget everything else. *You're the only one for me*, he said, and I believed it. Pierre was the only one who could make me feel better, and the only boy who ever whispered, *This is forever*.

That's all gone now, I remind myself. *There is no forever*.

"Vivian?" I hear from below me.

The Devil speaks. When I look down, I'm suspended from a rope ten feet in the air, bathed in bright light, and I can barely see Pierre standing below me, dressed as Don Juan.

"My character's name is Ines," I snap. "And you're Don Juan. So for once, try being professional, and stay in character."

"But I have to talk to you!"

"You've said enough already." Anger, hot as lava, shoots through me. I can feel myself tremble in my flying harness, and the cables holding me up rattle.

"Vivian?" the director calls up to me. "I need you to stay calm."

"I'm sorry it ever happened. But last night, when Sparrow and I were, you know," Pierre says, the sound of her name on his lips sawing me in half, "we heard something strange—"

Mary steps out of the shadows, her voice wrapping safely around me as she talks to the director. "Stop this. He's upsetting her."

"Pierre!" the director orders. "One more word and you're off the set!"

"Yes, sir." Pierre's defeated voice makes me feel a little better, and my shaking slowly subsides.

"Vivian?" the director asks me, sadness coating the edges of every word. "Are you ready?"

"Ready," I say. And it's the truth. I'm always ready for a movie shoot. It's like stepping out of reality for a minute, letting go and knowing something will catch you. The sad parts are still sad, but I get to call "Cut" to end the scene and walk away. Unfortunately, there isn't anything like that in real life. I would've yelled "Cut" months ago.

I'm headed back to my trailer, having successfully avoided Pierre, when I hear Mary's scream. I'd know that scream anywhere; despite her ability to kill a man in two seconds, she's terrified of spiders. Give her a full-blown samurai with a mean streak, she's fine, but pit her against a spider, and the eight-legged arachnid wins every time.

We have a deal: I'm in charge of smashing spiders, she's in charge of assailing stalkers, so with my heels clip-clapping against the hot asphalt, I jog the last few steps to my pink trailer. My two-story, custom-made pink trailer is blinking sunlight from every window. I push my thumb against the keypad beside the door, and the door slides open into my empty interview room, complete with vacant leather couches and hulking studio lights.

I rush past the interview room, bolt up the stairs, and run through the marble-tiled bathroom. When I get to my bedroom, I'm expecting to see Mary standing on a chair, a thing the size of her baby toe crawling on the floor beneath her, but she's just sitting on my bed, staring at my flat screen.

"Where's the spider?" I ask.

Mary's gasping for breath, like she's having an asthma attack. "No spider."

"Then what is it?" I ask, glancing around my pink chiffon-draped bedroom. Everything seems in place: the door to my walk-in closet is still slightly ajar; the half-drunk cappuccino rests on my nightstand, making a thick water ring on the mahogany.

"You know that DVD you gave me?" she says. "Well, I watched it and—"

"Breathe."

Mary takes one deep, shaky breath. "You need to see it."

"I don't wanna see it," I say, stepping closer to my nightstand and scowling at the milk now curdling up on the surface of my cappuccino. "That's why I gave it to you."

But Mary ignores me, focusing on the TV.

And that's when I find out I'm going to die.

Chapter Three

I DON'T WANT TO WATCH as the familiar scene from Mom's murder passes before me: the yellow CRIME SCENE tape, wrapped around the perimeter of the run-down apartment building, bleaching white as camera flashes hit it; the shattered streetlight outside the crumbling brick facade; the bloodstains on the second-story window. It's the same scene from Mom's *Etv! Memorial Special* that I swore I'd never watch again, except this time, the voice-over is different.

"Last night, Vivian Divine was found dead in an apartment in North Hollywood."

An ice-cold wind sweeps over me, making the hairs on my neck stand up.

"What did he say?" I ask Mary, chills running over my skin. She doesn't answer; her eyes are glued to the screen. I turn back to the TV, shivers slithering down my spine as a collage of pictures of me fills the screen, all wearing that same cereal box grin.

"Just six months after the death of her mother, Pearl Divine, the world mourns this tragic loss."

On TV comes the sorrow shot, the picture I couldn't get away from for the past half year. It goes straight to the heartstrings of America: me at my mother's funeral, wearing a black Chanel dress, glaring at my dad. At that time, nobody knew that twelve hours earlier he had a gun to his head. Or that I had found him, drunk off whiskey and delirious with grief, before the gun went off.

My Oscar picture flashes briefly onto the screen, and then fades away as the voice-over continues:

"November first will live on in history as the day the young starlet and recent Oscar nominee Vivian Divine was killed."

The camera zooms in on a grainy picture. It looks like a cell phone shot, blurry but unmistakable. I'm lying facedown in my own blood, a knife sticking straight through the *V* on my purple hoodie.

I sink down onto the bed, wrapping my arms around my knees. *It's exactly how Mom was killed. The same apartment building, the blood on the window, the knife through her back.* . . . I'm too stunned to breathe, and I feel like I'm falling into a deep hole, darkness surrounding me on all sides.

The hoodie I'm wearing, my purple one with a *V* across the back, suddenly feels threatening. Sweat breaks out across my skin, and I can't feel anything but the knife plunging into my back. My sweat stinks like blood, and—

"Vivian?"

My head snaps up. Mary has the same frightened look as when she wakes me screaming from a nightmare. I want to answer, but my voice is tied in a knot in my throat and I'm shaking so hard I can barely see the TV.

Then out of the corner of my eye, I see my filming schedule tacked to the wall of the trailer and something catches in my brain. *The video said I died on November 1.* My brain struggles to remember why that's so important. Then it slaps me. Hard. If today's October 28, that means I'm going to die . . . four days from now.

Everything starts to fade away. It's like I'm not here, in my trailer, in this body. A heavy numbness spreads over me and the room gets fuzzy. I want to look in a mirror to make sure I'm still here.

"Maybe it's just a stalker," I whisper. Hollywood's used to stalkers, and most of them are harmless. Everyone wants their fifteen minutes of fame. Just last month, some girl threatened suicide out of love for Pierre, and a guy followed Sparrow home swearing God ordered them to be together. "People will do anything for attention."

"For attention?" Mary says, and I know we're both thinking of the dangerous ones, like Mark David Chapman, who shot John Lennon, or the obsessed fan who locked Sparrow's cousin in his cellar for two days. "I think we have to consider the possibility," she says, and I'm already putting my hands over my ears, hoping to block out her next words, "that someone's coming after you."

"This isn't a movie, Mary. These kinds of things don't happen. Not in real life."

I could tell her about real life, where people just die, suddenly, for no reason, on a normal day. There's no great buildup—just one moment they're here, and the next they're gone.

"It's happened before," Mary whispers.

"To who?" I roll my eyes. Mary's watched every TV series under the sun. She's probably waiting for a detective to walk in with a piece of evidence gripped in a set of tweezers.

"I'll just go to the police," I continue. "They'll protect

me from this psycho, whoever it is."

Mary's eyes are choked with tears. They remind me of my cappuccino's curdled milk, thick swaths of liquid clinging to the surface.

"Did you hear me?" I say to Mary, raising my voice. "The police will protect me."

"I heard you," Mary says softly. "Your mother said the same thing."

Chapter Four

FEAR FLOODS INTO ME LIKE ice water.

Tears drip down Mary's cheeks and pool on the floor beneath her. That scares me even more, because in the two years of being side by side every second of every day, I've never seen her cry, not even at Mom's funeral. "I'm sorry," she says. "You were—you are—too young to know this."

"Is it about Mom's . . . passing?" I definitely can't say the M word. *Murder* means something heavier, like she could have been in pain or tortured, or worse.

"Before your mom . . . passed," Mary says, "she got a package in the mail."

"A package?" *Oh God. I don't want to know where this is going.*

"What was in the package?"

"A DVD. It was just like this one. It showed . . . how she died," Mary says. "Then three days later, she was found dead."

This can't be happening. "What did she do?" I ask.

"She went to the police. They said they'd protect her. But a few hours later she disappeared."

"And then?" *Don't tell me. I know the end to this story.*

"And then she was murdered."

Murdered. I still see Mom's white shawl stiff with blood, her shining blond curls splayed across the floor.

"Why didn't you tell me all this before?" Anger at Mary is filling me now, and anger feels good, better than fear.

"There's a lot you weren't told," Mary says. "We had to keep secrets. For your own protection."

"Protection against who?"

"The ones that killed your mother."

Mom's death started with a secret. A secret behind closed doors, hidden in angry words and fights sharp as swords.

I saw the secrets behind Mom's eyes. So did the press. They were waiting for the leak, but secrets don't leak; they explode.

My first understanding of secrets came in the form of a death threat, delivered a month before she disappeared. A crinkled piece of paper, hidden from me by my mom's shaking hands. And it said: "I'm coming for the girl."

When I asked Mom about it, she started shaking so violently Dad had to lead her away. But before they left, I saw his eyes. He didn't know any more than I did. Mom wouldn't hide anything from us—would she?

Then for a month, we didn't get another letter, so I thought it was over.

I was wrong.

The day before Mom disappeared, our mailbox was stuffed with letters. There must have been two hundred, shoved into every inch of the box. The postal service said they didn't deliver them, and the police were even less helpful. They couldn't do anything because the letters came from nowhere. From nobody. Mom wouldn't let me read them, but I saw that there was the same date on every letter. September 25. The day I was born.

My body is heavy and numb. I curl into a ball and bury myself in my covers, bundling the pink feather duvet over my head. "What do you think I should do?" I ask Mary from under the covers.

Under the thick material, her voice sounds muffled and wavy. "Hide somewhere safe for a few days. If nobody can find you, nobody can hurt you," she says. "That'll give us time to figure out who's after you."

"But what if we don't figure it out?"

"What else do you suggest we do?" Mary asks. "Go to the police? That's what your mother did. And look where she ended up."

Like I need a reminder. "But I can't disappear in the middle of shooting! Not during this movie!" It's true: the twisted love story between the murderous, demented Don Juan and his kidnapped young love, Ines, is one of the most famous stories in history and, if rumors are true, my most important role since my Oscar-nominated debut in *Abandoned*. "Can't I just hide at home?" I ask, glancing nervously around the trailer.

"They can find you there. You can't even leave your closet without being photographed."

Mary's right. Paparazzi and tourists hide along our fence every day, trying to get a shot of me. There are photos of me everywhere: in my room, eating breakfast, stepping out of my closet in my fifteenth wardrobe change of the day. And if the paparazzi can find me, anyone can.

"I'm not going anywhere," I say, flinging open my closet and rummaging through dozens of designer dresses until I find Mom's favorite stretchy green Pucci dress. It hasn't been dry-cleaned, so I can still smell her on it, like lying in a field of lavender. "Except home," I insist.

As I tug the dress over my round hips, I think about how Mom didn't run, leaving her family and career behind. Pride surges through me. Mom fought for us until the end. She wouldn't want me to run; she'd want me to stay, to fight.

But then again, she didn't run. And look what happened to her.

After glancing at myself in the mirror, I walk down the stairs and throw open the trailer door.

Flashes stun me from every side, popping in my face. Nearly blind, I stumble forward, fighting to keep my smile on. *Keep walking. This will end soon.* But the flashing only increases, and faces of reporters, their eyes hidden by shiny black cameras, appear and disappear in lightning strokes. I can't see anything as I stumble along, imagining a killer's face in every grasping, screaming journalist.

"Did you know about Pierre and Sparrow?" a reporter calls out, pushing a microphone in my face. I attempt to break out of the crowd, but someone grabs the hem of my dress. I try to paste on a bright smile, but my lips are trembling, so I'm half smiling, half frowning, and my waving hand feels disconnected from my body. I feel like I'm being sucked underwater by a surging, screaming undertow.

"How does it feel to be replaced?" a journalist asks. I know what he wants me to say, so he can splash my heartbreak all over his trash magazines, but I can't speak. My words waver, disappear.

"Did you and Pierre break up?" another reporter asks.

Break up? Until last night, Pierre had been the only person besides Mary who I could trust. He was the person I told all my secrets to, sometimes talking on the phone until the early hours of the morning. I had even told him my deepest secret: how I thought I could never feel happy again. *And now I never will.*

"Everybody, back up!" Mary yells, popping out of the trailer behind me, but the reporters just jostle closer. "I'll call security," she says.

It's too late. The press is already here.

Then I see, through the flashes, what drew them here. In the middle of the crowd are Pierre and Sparrow— together. *That's why all the paparazzi are here. To see the bloodbath.*

My skin bristles with anger. "What do you want?"

"We need to talk to you," Sparrow says, pushing through the reporters. Her whiny voice reminds me of the nights we used to stay up with Mary, listening to stories about first kisses and true love. Since Sparrow went to an all-girls school and I was homeschooled by a private tutor neither of us knew much about boys, until I started dating Pierre. *Before she stole him from me.* "It was a mistake," Sparrow says.

"Kissing my boyfriend was a mistake?" I shriek so loudly the reporters take a step back before lunging forward again. *Get it together. Never lose your temper in front of the camera.* I can see the headlines: *Teen Star Slaps Former Best Friend in Fit of Rage. Career Plunges.*

"V, please." Pierre leans toward me, placing his hand gently on my arm. He's as sexy as ever, with his dizzying blue eyes and his shock of white-blond hair. I see the past year of my life in his eyes: the way I felt when he sang my song, how we talked each other to sleep at night, the tremble in his lips when he kissed me. I automatically suck in my stomach—Pierre likes skinny girls—but I let it out again when I see his other hand entwined with Sparrow's. "There's something you should know—"

"I don't want to hear your excuses!" I pry Pierre's hand off my arm. The tears have broken through my wall now; they're streaming down my face, probably completely ruining my makeup. "You said you loved me," I mumble, just loud enough for him to hear.

Before he can respond, studio security surrounds the crowd and Mary whisks me off toward the limo.

"Vivian!" Pierre yells as I climb into the limo. "I need to tell you—"

I slam the door and his voice snaps into silence. *What do you need to tell me, Pierre? That when you said "forever" you meant "until someone better comes along"? Or that you never loved me in the first place?*

As Mary gets into the driver's seat, I curl up in the backseat, trying to get away from Sparrow and Pierre, and from the blackest hole in the universe: my broken heart.

I press my face up against the hard ridge between the backseats, where the leather's cool on my feverish skin, and focus on breathing in the smell of leather polish. I feel small and scared, like I'm drowning in water no one else can see.

The smell of Mom's lavender perfume suddenly washes over me, as strong as a pillow pressing down on my face. Then Mom's shaking hands holding the letter that said, "I'm coming for the girl," flashes through my mind. I bury my head deeper into the leather seats. *Why did they kill you, Mom? Is it my fault?*

"Vivian!" The voice sounds like it's coming from a great distance. "Vivian! What's wrong? Speak to me!"

The smell of leather polish fills my senses again, and all I hear is Mary calling my name from the front seat of the limo.

"Are you okay?" Mary asks. She's pulled onto the shoulder of the empty road and backed against a rock overhang so the paparazzi can't sneak up and take pictures from behind.

I must look like a lunatic. I sit up and uncurl my fists, feeling the stiff muscles of my hands. I'm suddenly grateful that Mary's in charge of driving me to the studio, because she knows how to avoid the press. *What if the paparazzi caught me like this? They'd say I was having a breakdown. And maybe they'd be right.*

"Have you talked to your dad about these feelings yet?" Mary asks.

I shake my head. *When have I talked to my dad about anything?*

As hard as I try to push it away, the guilt keeps coming back. Mary's always telling me it's not my fault, but it doesn't help—the feelings grab me like a fist, shaking me until my core rattles with pain.

When Mom first died, Mary suggested I see a therapist, but Dad doesn't believe in therapy. He's from the generation of men that thinks you should be able to cure yourself, just like he believes that "bootstraps were made so you could pull yourself up." *How many times have I heard that?*

"Let's just go home," I whisper, chewing nervously on my lower lip.

But before Mary can turn back around, a silver sedan pulls onto the shoulder, cornering us against the rock overhang. Someone gets out, leaving the blinding headlights on.

"Who's that?" I ask, putting my hand in front of my face to block the light.

"I don't know," Mary whispers. "But he's blocked us in." With our back bumper against the rocks, and the man standing against our front bumper, we can't move. It's too dark to see his face, but his spiky gray hair and black suit cut a sharp outline against the sky. Light streams around him, lighting him from behind like an evil archangel.

A rush of dizziness fills my head. *He's going to kill me here, on the side of the road.* A familiar terror is washing over me, like I'm locked inside a box, my muscles cramping from cold.

The man's lips are opening and closing, but with the doors closed, I couldn't hear him if he were screaming through a megaphone. *He's probably telling me he killed my mom, and now I'm going to die.* In slow motion, I watch the man pull a gun from his pocket and aim it at the windshield.

"Vivian! Get down!" Mary yells. She hits the gas, and the limo smashes into him. He catapults onto the hood, his face spreading out across the windshield. For a second, his eyes, one blue, one brown, stare straight at me. Then he flips over the roof and disappears from view. A streak of gold slides down the glass, catching on the windshield wipers.

Mary gets out of the limo, shoots me a look like an owner telling a dog to stay, then locks the door behind her. I lean against the back window, my forehead making a sweating moon in the glass.

As Mary searches the ground around the limo, bad endings of B horror flicks keep running through my head. I'm imagining his hand shooting out from beneath the limo, grabbing her ankle, and dragging her under. I picture her legs kicking the air, the sound of her bloodcurdling scream—

A knock on my window makes me jump. It's Mary. And she's holding an FBI badge.

Chapter Five

WHEN WE GET HOME, MARY ushers me up the grand staircase to my room, the clicking of my heels echoing through the empty house. After she locks the dead bolt on my bedroom door, she hands me the FBI badge, its shiny pendant faceup. "To Protect and Serve," the letters under the pendant say. *And to kill.*

"Vivian, that means—"

"The FBI tried to kill me." Pounding starts inside my head. I drop onto my canopied feather bed, too tired to stand. "What do we do?"

"We don't tell anybody," Mary says, "until we know who's after you. But for now, we need to think about other options."

"Other options?" I ask, scanning through my list of options: I could go to the police, like Mom did, but she ended up dead. I could call the FBI, but they might be trying to kill me. I could stay here and hope no one comes to kill me. Or I could hide. Go to a place where no one would ever find me.

"If I hid," I ask, "how long would I be gone?"

"Just for a few days," Mary says. "Until we figure out who is after you."

My chest tightens into a fiery ball. I feel like I'm burning from the inside out.

"Your dad and I tightened the security to protect you," Mary continues. "But if the police are involved, and the FBI . . . then it's not safe for you to be here."

"But even if we disappeared," I ask, "where would we go?"

Mary shakes her head. "You'll be safer going alone. If we're both gone, they might notice and come after you. But if I stay here and say you're sick, I can buy you some time before anyone notices you're missing."

"No," I say, shaking my head until it feels like it'll spin off my neck. "I'm not going anywhere alone." *Has she completely lost her mind?* I've never been anywhere alone. I have trainers, bodyguards, handlers to make sure I'm taken care of, that my every need is met. I've never even gone to the other side of L.A. alone. *But if Mary's right, could a few days save my life?* "If I went," I ask, "where would I go?"

"My friend Roberto builds safe houses for abused women, asylum seekers, anyone in real trouble. Six months ago, he helped me set up a safe house for your mom in Mexico, but she never made it."

We both know why, although neither of us says it: *If Mom hadn't trusted the police, if she had gone to the safe house instead, she might be alive today. If I don't go, will I end up the same way?* I take a few unsteady breaths. "So if I did go, how would I get there?"

"You'd have to go by bus," Mary says.

"By bus? To Mexico?" I shriek. "Don't people get, like, decapitated on buses? It happened in Canada. Some guy fell asleep and slash! Straight across the throat."

"But buses take cash, there are no names, no records. Even the police don't know who's on a bus."

I shiver. *Who do you trust if you can't trust the police?*

Operation Vivian Transformation makes me feel a little better. Mary cuts and dyes my hair, picks out an ugly black T-shirt and jeans from my character wardrobe, and finds me a pair of brown contacts, which I'm used to wearing, thanks to my months of demon-red contacts in *Zombie Killer*. Then instead of my pink Fendi suitcase, she hands me a horrid camo-print backpack and turns me around to look in the mirror. I'm shocked. I don't recognize myself.

Not at all.

"Not bad," I comment, momentarily forgetting my heart-stopping fear. I remember how Mom used to tell me never to leave the house without putting my "best face" on, and for once, I'm living up to that. I mean, I'm normally cute: big blue eyes, pouty lips, long copper curls. But this is gorgeous. My short black hair falls straight and glossy as a waterfall; my eyes are melting chocolate. "I'll call Dad and tell him what's happening," I add.

"What if they're tapping his phone?" Mary's face wrinkles with worry. "If these people think he knows where you are, they might force him to talk."

Force him. Like torture. My throat swells, making it hard to breathe. *If I get Dad involved, he could get hurt. Even killed.* I bite my lip hard enough to draw blood. *No way. I'm not bringing him into this.*

"Once you're safely out of the country, I'll call your dad and let him know you're okay," Mary says, pulling a piece of paper out of her purse. "These directions will get you to Roberto," she continues. "And call me every day, but only on the number I programmed in. The phones could be tapped."

"All right." I'm getting more nervous by the second, sweat making my hands so slippery I almost drop my über-ugly backpack.

"Most importantly," Mary says, "don't tell anyone who

you are. If anyone recognizes you, and knows they can get a ransom for you . . ." She shivers. I do too. I've seen the TV specials, where girls disappear and never come back.

I feel shattered, ready to break apart at the seams. I throw the bag over my shoulder and take a step toward the door. When I look back at Mary, it's like I'm looking down a long tunnel leading to my past.

Chapter Six

BY THE TIME I TRANSFER buses in Tijuana, it's almost three in the morning. Although the border crossing was easy (they barely glanced at the fake passport Mary gave me), the skin around my throat tingles from five hours of sitting in terror, waiting for my head to be sliced off at the neck. I'm breathing in shallow gasps, feeling disease-causing germs lining my lips, my tongue. *They'll find my body on the dirty bus floor, dead from some airborne disease.* Every bone in my body wants to run screaming off the bus. *But if I get off the bus, they might be waiting to kill me.*

Tears threaten to spill out of me, but I push them back and make myself sit on the edge of a plastic seat, sticky from ground-in gum, and try to avoid direct contact with my skin. *Think Mexican beaches, massages, the rolling surf.*

Eventually the terror of the last twenty-four hours catches up with me, and I can barely keep my eyes open. To keep myself awake (and my head securely on my neck), I pull Mary's directions out of my pocket again. The words blur beneath my lowering eyelids, but it doesn't matter: by this time, I've read the note so many times the words are bludgeoned into my memory.

> *V,*
>
> *Buy a cash ticket for the 1203 bus to Tijuana, then transfer to the 606 bus to Rosales. From there, take any ferry to Isla Rosales. Roberto will meet you on the dock. He'll be wearing a cowboy hat. He'll hide you for as long as you need—*

My eyes are starting to close. I wrench my head back up and focus on the directions again.

> *—which hopefully won't be long. Remember, don't tell anyone who you are or where you're going. Please take care of yourself, and know I'll be there soon.*
>
> *XO,*
>
> *Mary*
>
> *PS: Destroy this note after reading it.*

My eyelids have drooped so low that the words are blurring together. I shove the directions into the bag at my feet, and let my eyes close. Exhaustion takes over and I crash headfirst into sleep.

Screaming wrenches me from my nightmare. My dream washes over me again, taking my breath away. I'm stuck in a black box. It's baking hot, and I'm pounding the top with my fists, but nobody comes. I bite my lip to stop screaming, but it just gets louder. *I'm not the one screaming. It's coming from outside the bus.*

Outside my window, dozens of dark-skinned women are standing around the bus driver, yelling in Spanish and pointing to smoke billowing out of the engine. The bus driver looks scared, like these ladies are going to beat him to death with their hard little purses. *Is this when the decapitation happens?*

Across the deserted horizon, the sun is rising over the cacti, reminding me that it's now October 29—and that I might only have three more days to live. I want to curl into a ball and never come out, but the bus is getting so hot I make myself climb out into the scorching desert sunlight.

"How long until the next bus?" I ask as I approach the group of women, raising my voice and slowing down each word. An ancient lady shakes her head, her skin sagging around her two remaining teeth.

She doesn't speak English? What do I do now? I flash back to my half-hour Spanish tutoring session with Mary. Unfortunately, "Where's the bathroom?" and "I'm looking for a man in a big hat" won't help in this situation.

"Bus," I say, pointing at the smoking engine. "No work?" I raise my voice and announce, "Does anybody speak English?"

The women all shake their heads, and I suddenly remember that I have my disposable cell phone in my bag. *I'll just call the number Mary programmed in for me, tell her I'm stuck, and have her order me a car. I'll be lounging on the beach in no time.*

I quickly climb onto the bus, nurturing visions of the local Four Seasons picking me up in an air-conditioned private car. I'm so lost in my daydream of a cold pool and chocolate-dipped strawberries that I almost pass my seat, but thanks to the gum ground into the plastic, I find it. But when I reach under the seat, my bag is gone.

Terror jolts through me as my hand slides over empty ground. *My bag has to be here.* It has everything in it: my phone, my money, my fake passport. *This isn't happening. Not now. Not to me.*

Adrenaline shoots through me, and I drop down to my knees and look under the seat, breathing in the smell of urine and disinfectant. I run my hands over the floor, hoping I missed it, that the tacky camouflage is, well, camouflaged, but nausea rises in my stomach, and fear wraps its way through my body. *Someone stole my bag.*

I jump up and race down the aisle, frantically checking all the overhead bins. *It has to be here!* I pull plastic bags, soccer balls, bottles of Fanta out of the bins until there's a mound of supplies up and down the bus. It looks like a hurricane has hit here. *Still no bag.* Then above the last row, I pull out a bundle of thick material. But when it comes tumbling out, it's a red soccer jersey with the word MEXICO printed across the back.

My knees turn to jelly, and I slouch against the back wall, my world crumbling around me. *Please, God. I'll forgive Sparrow. Even Pierre. Just this one tiny miracle, please.* Those tears that never come threaten to spill down my cheeks, and the bus gets bleary. I blink, feeling the contacts scratch against my corneas. I pluck them out and toss them on the floor, and then bury my face in the jersey's thick red cloth.

"*Eso es mío,*" a voice says from behind me.

I don't bother to turn around. I feel like a cigarette someone stamped out on the floor. I have no idea what he's saying, and tears are running down my face now, soaking the red jersey.

"*Eso es mío,*" the voice says again.

Can't you see I want to be alone! But he's still there, so I reluctantly turn around.

Standing in front of me is the sexiest guy I've ever seen.

His eyes are a rugged green, his black hair shaggy on his shoulders. His cargo pants hang off his slim hips, and a white undershirt clings to his chest. My personal trainer would kill for his body. *How could I have fallen for Pierre when there are men in the world like this?*

"*Hola.*" I'm completely tongue-tied. I try to smile at him, but it's like my mouth has frozen.

"*¿Esa es mi camisa?*" He points to my chest. I shake my head, not understanding, and grip the wet jersey tighter.

He leans forward, coming close enough to me to touch. "My shirt?"

I flush a crimson red. I've got his soccer jersey balled up against my chest, covered in tears and snot. *Can this get any more embarrassing?*

I release my death grip on his jersey and hand it to him, and he pulls it over his white undershirt. To my horror, his chest is splotched with wet stains, but he doesn't even notice. *Maybe girls cry on his shoulder all the time.*

"What are you looking for?" he asks, eyeing the disaster I've created. His deep voice is tinged with a slight Mexican accent.

"I lost my bag."

"I guess so," he says, clicking his tongue against the roof of his mouth. "So what was in the bag?"

What wasn't in the bag? "My money. My phone. My passport."

He whistles under his breath. "Probably long gone.

Hard cash? Gone. And American passports are like gold around here." He adds, smirking at me, "Not a smart move, princess."

What a jerk! I lost my entire life and he calls me a princess and tells me I'm an idiot? This day is getting worse every minute. I think of my options: walk hours through the middle of nowhere until I get to the border and make them let me back in, probably straight into my killer's hands, search every passenger head to toe, or have someone else find my bag. *Perfect.*

"Will you find my bag for me?" I ask, putting on my most helpless look. It isn't hard: the damsel-in-distress role is one I know well. People are always ready to save me from a mistake on set—an unruly costume change, or a forgotten line in my script. Everyone loves a damsel in distress, and if there ever was one, it's me right now.

"Me? Why me?"

"Well, someone on the bus stole it. And you speak Spanish."

He rolls his eyes. "I don't even know your name."

"We don't have time for this." I'm getting impatient, and when I get impatient in my world, heads roll, people are fired, shoots are canceled. *But what happens here?*

"I have all the time in the world." He leans against a bus seat, like he's lounging on a beach somewhere, waiting for his massage. "So, do you have a name?"

Good question. Suddenly I can't remember the name on

my fake passport, even though Mary made me say it over and over until it sounded natural. Isabel? Ingrid? "Ines," I say, just loud enough for him to hear. I figure that's the closest to real I'm gonna get. And I'm so used to hearing it on set, I might just answer to it. If I'm lucky.

"Okay, Ines. I'm Nicolas, but my friends call me Nick," he says. "You'd better stick with Nicolas."

"Okay, Nicolas. Enough small talk. Get me my bag."

"*Bueno*, princess," he says. "Just don't ask for any more favors."

I follow Nicolas off the bus. Around us, the desert stretches out for miles, broken only by prickly cacti and tumbleweeds. When he walks up to the group of women, they immediately stop talking and look him over from head to toe.

"*¿Quién se llevó la mochila de la gringa?*" he asks, pointing to me. The women all glare at me for a second, their anger searing me like a hot wind.

"What did you say to them?" I demand when he returns to the bus.

"I said, 'Give back the bag you stole,'" Nick says, "'or the gringa will kill you.'"

"You did not!" I snap. "Do you at least have a phone?"

He pulls two pieces of a shiny black phone out of his pocket. "Broken. I dropped it in the station."

Who better to steal a phone than someone who just broke theirs? I scan every ragged tear in his clothes, the grime under his fingernails, his shaggy hair that so obviously needs a haircut. "You know what? I think you stole it!"

I regret the words as soon as they're out of my mouth. All the light drops out of his eyes, and his face becomes hard, unreadable. "What did you just say?"

"You heard me," I say, but softer, hoping to retract the words.

He glares at me as he pulls his pockets inside out and dumps their contents on the ground. A torn bus ticket, a pocketknife, and a pack of Chiclets roll in the dirt at our feet. "Satisfied? Or do you want to check my shirt again?" He grabs his pocketknife, stuffs it in his side pocket, and then stomps off.

I watch him storm up the road, getting smaller every second, and a knot forms in my stomach. "Where are you going?" I call after him.

"None of your business," he yells back.

"But when does the next bus come?"

I can't see his lips move, but the wind carries his words back to me. "Next week."

I hate asking for help. Luckily, I never have to. A team of specialists is paid to take care of my every need, to anticipate what I might want and have it prepared ahead of time. If they don't have the right brand of mango lip balm ready for me after a shoot, they're done.

But this isn't quite so simple. I'm standing on a dusty road in the middle of nowhere, feeling more alone than I ever have in my life. Dry grass and cacti spread out as far as I can see. Besides Nicolas, who is pacing back and forth with his thumb out, the word MEXICO on the back of his red soccer jersey wavering in the heat, everyone from the bus is so far up the road that they have almost disappeared into the dust.

A hot, itchy hour passes before I see a thin line of dust rise in the distance. As it gets closer, I can make out a large yellow pickup truck with a blue plastic tarp tented on poles over the back. There's black smoke coming out of it, coloring the sky, and it sounds like something is beating it to death.

As the truck pulls up beside me, the driver leans out his window, his mustache curling up on the edges. "*¿A dónde vas?*"

I know what Mom would do. She'd say, *Leave it to the universe,* and jump in the truck, and then amuse the driver by telling a story about how she fell in love with my dad on the set of *Medusa's Revenge* and got married three months later. By the end of the story, the driver would adore her, but I'm not Mom, so I shake my head, sure that he just asked me if he could cut out my kidneys and discard my lifeless body on the side of the road. I've seen this movie before: the organ trafficker makes thousands and the girl always ends up dead.

Farther up the road, Nicolas holds his hand out to the organ traffickers and the truck pulls to a slow stop. As my stomach growls like a rabid animal, I weigh the options: *Lose a kidney or starve to death?* I swallow my spit to soothe my throat, and as the truck pulls away, I swallow my pride, running after it at full speed.

When I'm twenty feet back, waving my arms frantically and pumping my legs as hard as I can, I catch my toe on a rock and sprawl, face-first, into the dust.

This is the worst day of my life.

But then the truck grinds to a stop, and Nicolas gestures to me. I pull myself off the ground, my hands tingling with droplets of bright red blood. As I walk the last few feet to the truck, I study Nicolas's rugged face, afraid he's going to pull away at the last minute and leave me stranded again. But he doesn't. He just puts out one hand and pulls me up onto the truck.

"Come on, princess," he says. "Just don't bleed on me."

Chapter Seven

AS SOON AS I CLIMB onto the back, the truck jerks forward. There are no seats back here, just two wooden benches lining the sides. A mariachi band is crammed onto the benches, knee to knee, their shiny instruments gleaming so brightly they hurt my eyes. On the floor, a barefoot little girl is playing with a lamb, her grin exposing her missing front teeth, and a lady with a long braid is nestled beside her.

"Thanks for stopping," I say, wedging myself onto the truck bed between Nicolas and the tailgate. It's tied together with rope, ready to burst open and send me tumbling into the street. "Can't I sit in front?"

He shakes his head, his eyes narrowing into small slits.

"Okay." I sigh. "Look, I'm sorry I called you a thief."

"You should be," he says, turning to face me. "So where are you going, princess?"

"Rosales," I say uneasily, unsure of how much I should tell him. "Can I be there by tomorrow?"

"You're on Mexican time now. Everything takes a little longer," he warns me. "And my chauffeur is off duty today," he says sarcastically. "So don't expect a miracle."

Apparently we're done talking, because Nick leans his head back and closes his eyes. His shaggy black hair may be begging for a haircut, but it falls in soft curls around his face, and his ragged red jersey fits snugly across his well-built—

"BAAA!" I look up, and the little girl is standing over me, settling the squirming lamb into my lap. I shriek, trying to backpedal away from the lamb's tiny legs kicking into my thighs. I've never been around a wild animal before, and I have to force myself not to shove it off my lap. "Is it s-safe to hold him?" I ask.

"You might ruin your nails," Nick quips, so I swallow the lump in my throat and push down the voice inside me screaming that the beast's going to bite a rabid hole in my leg. *It's safe. He won't bite me.* I gingerly touch the lamb's fuzzy pink ears, and he licks me with his rough tongue. "What's his name?" I ask.

The little girl shakes her head, and I wonder if *dinner* is the right answer. *I'm gonna call him Honey.*

"Why are you going to Rosales?" Nick asks me, letting Honey lick the back of his hand. "I can tell you're not a girl who'd cross the border, well, ever."

To meet a man who will protect me from the people who murdered my mother? Other than that, I don't know what to say. "Um . . . I'm visiting my uncle Roberto."

"So you're here for Los Muertos?"

I nod. Whatever Los Muertos is, I'm here for it. *I just hope it's not human sacrifice.*

"You have no idea what I'm talking about," Nick says.

I shrug.

"Los Muertos? The Day of the Dead?" Nick scoffs. "It's only the biggest holiday of the year! Do they teach you nothing at your rich American school?"

"I knew that," I say, lying through my teeth. "And I don't go to a rich American school."

I focus on the mariachi players crammed onto both benches, their red-and-gold-embroidered suits twinkling like jewels under the sun, glad that I could tell the truth for once. Or half-truth, anyway. I've never actually been to school. Mom always insisted I have a private tutor, a stodgy professor from England who fills my head with boring information for four hours every day. But I've acted in enough high school movies to know that gym clothes itch and cafeterias have rotten food and you have to fit all your stuff in one tiny locker. *What else do I need to know?*

"Oh, really?" Nick says. "So you're just a poor girl who stole some rich girl's shoes?" He points to my shoes, and a self-satisfied smirk stains his face.

I glance down, past my cheap black T-shirt, past my totally tacky faded jeans, to my sparkling white sneakers with the gold G on the sides. *I can't believe I forgot to change out of my Gucci sneakers.* "Those are hand-me-downs." *From Mr. Gucci.*

"Whatever," Nick says. "So you're what? Three years younger than me? Fifteen, maybe?"

"Sixteen," I correct him. *When I was fifteen my mom was alive, and I was safe at home with a boyfriend and a best friend.* "Sixteen sucks," I add, surprising myself by my honesty.

"Pardon me, princess." Nick rolls his eyes. "Baby's all grown up now."

"I can handle myself!" I snap, not at all sure that's true. *In the studio, yes. On the back lot, definitely. But in the real world?* I stare at the mariachi players. They are barefoot, the fringes of their gold mariachi pants ragged around their ankles. *Is this the real world everyone's talking about?* "What about you?" I ask Nick, desperate to get the attention off me.

"Me? I'm done with school," Nick says, "and unlike some people"—he gives me a meaningful glance—"I *work* for a living."

"What's that supposed to mean?"

"You just don't look like the kind of girl who *works*," he says. He picks up my manicured fingers and runs his index finger over them. "More like the girl people like me work *for*."

I shake his hand off mine. "I work," I say.

"Oh yeah? Doing what?"

I think of how exhausting it is to film the same scene dozens of times, and of the weary, sleepless nights preparing for a part or memorizing a script. But I can't tell him about my job, so I just look away.

"That's what I thought," Nick says bitterly.

"You don't know me," I snap. "So don't act like you do."

"You're right, I don't. And maybe I don't want to," Nick says.

"There's no *maybe* about it on my part," I respond. He turns his back to me, and I inch as far away from him as I dare, without falling out the back of the truck.

Several hours later, my back aching and my skin itchy with dust, the truck stops in front of an old stone church. It's beautiful, but in that "I'm going to be crushed to death by falling stones" kind of way.

"Father García lets travelers sleep here. It's the last stop before the mountains," Nick explains. "And the last chance for you to run your princess butt home."

I ignore him, focusing instead on the sound of "last

stop." It sounds like a cue for getting my personal will in order. "We don't have time to stop," I say, imagining missing Roberto and dying in an alley at the hands of a vicious gang. "We need to get to Rosales by morning."

"You know what I need? For you to stop complaining."

"I'm not complaining!"

Nick shakes his head. "I'll take you as far as I can," he says. "Trust me."

"Yeah, right," I mutter. I hate when people say "trust me." Pierre said "trust me" in the same breath he said "forever." I picture Pierre and Sparrow kissing, their arms wound tightly around each other. I shove my thumbnail into the soft flesh of my index finger. *I bet he doesn't even miss me.*

I force Pierre out of my head and follow Nick across the small, dark courtyard to the church. It looks familiar. I've seen this church before, I realize, on the studio's back lot. It's the "Traditional Mafia Church" set. Usually directors film shoot-'em-up scenes here, or drug deals gone bad. Either way, someone dies. I can think of nothing else as Nick opens the door for me, and I go in.

I've never seen so much gold in my life. Seriously. Not in Mom's jewelry drawers, or at Tiffany, or even on all of Rodeo Drive. The walls, ceiling, and altar are solid gold.

I'm shocked. There's enough gold in this church to buy

Beverly Hills, but I had to ride all the way here in a nearly broken-down truck with people who can't afford shoes.

"What are you doing?" I ask as Nick kneels beside what looks like a birdbath and dips his fingers in. I've never met anyone religious, except Scientologists. *But they believe we are descendants of aliens, so that doesn't count, does it?*

"Sign of the cross," Nicks says, looking at me like I've been hiding under a large, ignorant rock for years. He moves his thumb in a cross shape over his chest. "My mom raised me in the church."

"And now?"

"Now?" He drops his hand from his chest. "She'd be disappointed in who I am now."

Before I can ask him why, he walks through a doorway to the left of the altar. *What would Mom think of me? Running for my life, trusting a complete stranger to get me to safety?* I hurry up the aisle, passing the bright gold altar. *She'd tell me to trust the universe to take care of me, and she'd call me the Holy Fool, who makes the world smile as she leaps off the cliff. Then again, Mom had a way of believing everything would turn out all right, even when it didn't.* I step into the room just left of the altar, where people are laying out brightly colored blankets across the concrete floor.

This is where we're staying? He's got to be kidding! This room looks like a prison cell. The walls are bare concrete, and a single bulb dangles from the ceiling. There's a cot against the back wall, and hanging above it is a giant, multicolored tapestry of the Crucifixion.

"It's perfect for you," I say, trying not to let a grimace cross my face. "Which way to my room?"

Nick raises his eyebrows, his look stern and disapproving. "They want you to take the bed," he says. "You're their guest. It would be an insult to say no."

By the time I'm settled onto the disappointingly hard cot, having fluffed the thin pillow and estimated the thread count of the sheets (150, tops), the whole room is asleep. There's a melody of snores in different tunes, and although I'm exhausted, I can't make myself sleep.

I watch Nick lying on the floor beside my bed. His eyelids are moving gently in sleep, his normally hard face relaxed, almost angelic compared to his bitter, caustic self when he's awake. *Is his mom disappointed in his stupid machismo attitude? Or just because he doesn't go to church anymore?* I've finally decided that it must be his bitter attitude when two sharp voices break the night.

"*¿Dónde está?*"

"*¿Quién?*"

Nobody wakes up. The snoring continues, but the sharp voices, coming from somewhere outside the room, are ringing in my ears. *Great. I'll never get to sleep now.*

Soon the voices sound angrier, one deep and gravely, the other high and pleading. I want to wake Nick, but he'd just make fun of me and tell me what a self-centered princess I am. If I were home, I'd wake Mary, sure it was two journalists sneaking over the fence. But Mary's not here, and it's probably just town drunks anyway. *But what if they're reporters?*

Don't be a fool, Vivian. Just go to sleep. I press my thin pillow over my ears, but I can still hear their voices burrowing into me, and I know I'll never sleep until I'm sure the paparazzi haven't found me. So, feeling like a scared kid, I step off the cot and sneak through the sleeping people to the back of the church.

At the entrance to the church, a black-robed figure looms in the open doorway. His back is to me, and the light from the moon pours over his shoulders, illuminating the gold cross stitched across his robe.

I can't see much of the other man, except his giant black silhouette cutting across the darkness. The church doorway slices off half his head, so he must be over seven feet tall, and I can't see his face, since it's submerged in the dark night. *Not that I want to.*

"*¿Dónde está la muchacha?*" the man growls.

His voice presses into me on both sides, and it feels like the concrete walls are caving in on me.

When the priest finally speaks back, his voice is small and begging. "*No sé. Y no quiero morir.*"

Isn't this when the priest pulls out a string of garlic and a big silver cross, and burns a hole through the undead's chest?

The man rubs a gun across the priest's cheeks, down to his chin, and then slowly up his nose to end in a point in the center of his forehead. *"Confiese or te mato."*

Something drips onto the floor around the priest's legs. It cradles the moonlight like liquid silver as it runs between the pews, and the small church fills with the smell of urine.

The man cocks the gun, and when he speaks, his voice sends chills through me. *"La niña,"* the man repeats, like he's bored with the situation, and would rather just kill him already. *"¿Dónde está?"*

While the priest quietly weeps, I hold my nose as the liquid snakes down the aisle, carrying the smell of the priest's terror toward me. The man keeps speaking Spanish in his dead, monotonous tone, except when he says the two words I fear most:

Vivian Divine.

Chapter Eight

AFTER HEARING MY NAME, I duck behind the altar, and I'm too afraid to move for over an hour. Even after the gunman leaves, I stay frozen in place, my eyes peeled open as the priest gets a rag and cleans the urine off the floor on his hands and knees. *How did that man know I was here? What does he want from me?* Those questions repeat endlessly in my mind until the priest folds the dirty rag and leaves the church, closing the front door softly behind him.

I sneak back into the other room and force myself to close my eyes on the hard little cot. *I can't handle this,* I repeat to myself, clutching the cheap cotton mattress with tight fists. *I should just go back to L.A. and take my chances. It might be better than this.*

The morning finally comes, after hours of alternating between sweat-soaked fear, my eyes pinned open, and deep, exhausted sleep, plagued by nightmares.

"Ines?" Nick's voice hits me at the same time the smell of coffee fills my senses. I sit up on the cot, my back stiff from the thin mattress. *It was just a nightmare.* I pick up the lukewarm cup of coffee on the floor beside my cot, already feeling a little better.

"You made it through your first night of poverty?" Nick sneers. "How'd you like it on the other side?"

I shrug my stiff shoulders, the sound of the man growling my name rolling over me. *What if he's still here?* My coffee spills over the side of the cup and splashes on the floor.

"You okay?" Nick actually sounds slightly concerned, and the sound of his voice helps chase away the memory of the man's low growl, the smell of urine, the knife-sharp edges of my real name.

"I'm okay," I say. *What am I supposed to say? Somebody wants to kill me? I've been lying to you about who I am?*

I take a long drink of the bitter coffee, and it dribbles out of my mouth and runs down my chin.

"Somebody call the servants," he says, and claps his hands twice. *So much for concern.*

I wipe my dripping chin with my tacky black T-shirt. "Shut up." I scowl.

Across the room, the woman with the long braid opens

a woven basket, and the little girl bounds across the room toward her, the baby lamb at her feet. The woman hands the girl a tinfoil package, and then calls across the room to Nick.

"*¿Tienes hambre?*" she asks, shooing the baby lamb away from her ankles.

"*Sí,*" Nick calls back.

"What'd she say?" I ask him. "And what did you say yes to?"

"So you know the word for yes," he says. "That's a start."

I glare at him.

The little girl pads across the room and drops the tinfoil package in Nick's lap.

"*Gracias,*" Nick says, and she squeals in shy pleasure as she dashes back to her mom's side. Nick quickly unwraps the tinfoil package, revealing two corn tacos with something green oozing out the sides, and hands me one of them. "Guacamole," he says when I look at it suspiciously. "What, are you afraid to eat it?"

"Um, yeah. It's from a *stranger*," I point out. *How do I know she's not trying to poison me?*

"Never mind," Nick mutters under his breath. "I'll eat them both." But when he tries to take the poisonous green taco back, my traitorously hungry stomach wins out, and I stuff it in my mouth and devour it in two bites. It's creamy and crunchy and salty, and gone way too fast.

"I want another," I insist, holding my palm out for the other one.

"You want *mine* too?" Nick asks angrily. "Do you ever stop wanting?" He rolls his eyes in my direction, but then his face quickly transforms into a smile. "Sure, *no problema*," he says, peeling his taco open and laying it flat on my upturned palm.

Inside, in a straight line across the tortilla, are a dozen dead crickets.

I think I'm going to puke. "You jerk!" I snap, ignoring how everyone in the room is turning to watch me. "Were there crickets in my—"

"Local specialty," Nick interrupts. "But they tasted good, didn't they?"

I glare at his grinning face, summoning up the right words for how much I hate him, when the priest steps into the doorway.

The room drops into complete silence. My anger at Nick dies in my throat, and fear surges through me as I remember the priest on his hands and knees, wiping up the urine after the man finally left.

"*Buenos días*," the priest says, his voice sounding much prouder than it did last night.

"*Buenos días*," the little girl says, breaking the silence. "*Gracias.*"

The priest nods as the room rings with a chorus of

"*gracías, gracías.*" He bows his head slightly as each person steps up to say thank you. But after the priest nods politely to Nick, he turns to me. The smile instantly slides off his face and his jaw tightens into a quivering line. His previously compassionate eyes turn hard, unreadable.

"*Gracías?*" I say, hoping the smile returns to his face. It doesn't. Instead, he continues to stare at me, his forehead wrinkling in anger. Slowly, every person in the room turns and stares at me.

"*¿Cómo te llamas?*" the priest asks me.

My mouth feels sticky and dry. I shift uncomfortably, averting my gaze to Nick. He's glaring at the priest, his fists curling up by his sides.

"*¡Estás en peligro y estás poniendo toda esta gente en peligro!*" the priest says, moving so close to me I can smell his coffee breath.

"What's he saying?" I ask Nick, my voice trembling.

"Don't worry about it," Nick says. "He's just a crazy old man."

Now everybody's staring at me. "Nick? What's going on?"

Nick throws the priest another sharp look before translating for me. "He says you're in danger, and that you're endangering us all by being here."

Black edges into my vision as my legs strain to hold me up. *Don't pass out now.* The priest bursts into another rapid litany of Spanish, nodding at Nick to translate. Nick glares at the priest before turning to me.

"He says you have to leave now and never return," Nick says. "He says you'll be the death of us all."

It feels like a fist is closing around me, tightening until I can hardly breathe. *They've found me. I'm trapped here, and these people are trapped with me.* The priest is still glowering at me, but there's more fear than anger in his stare. *Who was he talking to last night?* People are backing away from me as if I've caught a contagious disease. The girl's mother shoots knives with her angry glare, and the mariachi band mirrors her expression.

"*¡Vete!*" she yells at me.

"*Por favor te marchas,*" the driver says, pointing to the door.

My eyes are filling with tears. I'm standing in front of a firing squad, and they're yelling directions I can't understand.

Trying not to cry and failing miserably, I walk as fast as I can out of the room. Nick's words echo through the room behind me, getting louder until he's practically shouting. I can only imagine what he's saying about me: how he knew I was evil all along, how he'd tried to get rid of me but I followed him onto the truck, begging for him to save my pathetic life. *Of course Nick hates me. I put all those people in danger. Everyone could have died because of me.*

I run up the aisle and out of the bright gold church, letting the door bang closed behind me. As I emerge into the
hot air, I wipe my tears off with the back of my hand; white
streaks run down my grimy fist.

When I reach the end of the courtyard, I glance back at
the church, imagining people with pitchforks chasing me.
Is that how it ends, with a pitchfork in my back?

The courtyard's still empty, but I hurry up the road
anyway, hoping I'm walking toward Rosales. Dust swirls
around my feet, coating my shoes and ankles in a layer of
itchy brown powder. *I have to get to Rosales. I have to find Roberto
and get to the safe house before that man finds me.*

Behind me, a door creaks open. Footsteps pound across
the courtyard.

"Ines!" Nick yells.

If he's coming to say good-bye, he can keep it. I continue walking,
watching the dust add layers to my dirty skin.

"Wait for me!" he yells.

So you can tell me to go away, like everyone else? I walk faster,
spitting my words behind me. "I'm going to Rosales."

Nick catches up to me, grabs my arm with his cold fingers, and pulls me to a stop. "I know the way."

I wriggle my arm out of his grasp. "I'm gonna be the
death of you, remember?"

"That old fool thought you were someone else," Nick
says. *Is he trying to make me feel better?*

"And if you're wrong?"

"Don't worry about me. I can take care of myself," Nick says. "Besides, you can't go alone. You'd never survive out here without me."

We've been walking this dirt road for hours, with nothing but the occasional tree breaking the endless brown horizon, and my feet hurt like they've been run over by a train. Spying a boulder on the roadside, I stop and rest my aching soles.

"How much further?" I ask.

"Tired already, princess?" Nick says, stopping a few feet ahead of me and looking back.

"Stop calling me that!"

"Is it not true?" Nick asks innocently, and then raises his voice to a higher pitch. "I can't touch a lamb! I don't want to sit in the back of a truck! I lost my bag and I can't find it myself! Give me a break." He shakes his head and continues to walk up the road, kicking the dusty ground with his feet. "Coming?"

"Nope." I let myself sink to the ground and lean against the boulder. My jeans are immediately coated with a light brown dust. "Not with you."

Nick stops again. He turns around, but he doesn't make a move to come back and get me. "Is any of that not true?" he asks.

I jump to my feet, my Gucci sneakers kicking up dirt. "I *did* hold the stupid lamb!" I yell at him. "And I sat in the back of the truck, even though it was dirty and disgusting!"

"Dirty *and* disgusting?" he mocks.

I stomp my feet into the dirt, and the flying dust makes me sneeze. "I don't know how you live down here," I say, covering my face with my sweaty elbow and sneezing into it, "but at home, we don't make our guests eat *crickets!*" I start hiking up the road, cursing all the four-letter words I know under my breath.

Nick just whistles as he watches me go by. "Nice words for a fancy lady."

"You made me use them!" I say over my shoulder.

In two large steps, he catches up to me, grabbing my elbow and yanking me to a stop. "I didn't *make* you do anything," he says. "Don't blame your petty problems on me."

Petty problems? Anger races through me, and I remember the judo move I learned for the all-night shoot of *Zombie Killer*. *I'll show you petty problems.* I wrap my hand around his right wrist and twist as hard as I can. He yelps, his eyes widening in surprise, and he drops my arm. I storm past him up the road, and this time, he backs up a bit as I pass him by.

I've lost track of time by now. Everything looks the same— dry and deserted and kind of . . . vacant. And since Nick and I aren't talking, everything sounds the same, like stale silence, and I'm so thirsty I can feel only the dry itchiness of my throat.

Not a single car has come by, and I'm thinking maybe the apocalypse has come, that humanity has been wiped off the earth or something, when we turn a corner, and there's a dumpy little taco stand on the roadside. Beside the rusty taco stand is a red cooler and a single card table, shaded by a ratty blue tarp. I have no idea who his customers are, but the old, blind man looks like he's been waiting for us.

Nick speaks to the man in Spanish for a moment, and then turns to me. "Taco?"

I shake my head. "Water."

Nick opens the cooler, and inside there are a few orange sodas. He hands one to me, and I pop it open and drink it half down in one breath.

"Take it easy," Nick says, and I drag it away from my lips. "*Dos tacos*," he says to the blind man, who nods at him, pulls a package of stuff out of the cooler, and drops it all on the grill. "You need to eat," Nick says.

"How do you know what I need?"

Nick sighs.

"But thanks for this," I say, gesturing to my orange soda. I pull out a plastic chair and drop into it. "Don't you have to pay?"

"He knows my cousin Antonio," Nick says. "He'll pay him later."

"Are we far from your cousin's house?"

"We're only half a mile away," Nick says. "If you can make it that far, Antonio will drive us to Rosales."

"I can make it." I glare at him, secretly hoping I really can make it to Antonio's house without lying down and dying of exhaustion by the roadside. "I told you, I can—"

"Take care of yourself, right," Nick says. "You couldn't take care of yourself if it punched you in the face."

"If you really don't want to be here," I say, "you can just point the way for me."

Nick shakes his head. He stands up, retrieves two tacos from the blind man's extended hand, and stuffs one in his mouth. "You'd starve to death. Or get eaten by animals. Or something equally *dirty and disgusting*," he says, taking down the second taco before he sits back down. "We take care of each other, even people we don't like. That's how we *do it down here*."

I take another long swallow of orange soda. "What's your problem with me?"

He wipes his mouth, balls up the napkin, and throws it into the metal trash can. "You're a spoiled brat. You have no problems," Nick says. "You think your life's so tough, but your rich mommy and daddy take care of everything for you." He snatches my orange soda from my hand, takes the last sip, and tosses it into the trash. "You don't know what real pain is."

I can't answer for a minute. *Is that really what he thinks of me?* I wipe my mouth, stuff the napkin in my pocket, and stand up. "If that's what you think, fine. But you're wrong." My voice is shaking, and I'm glad the old man is blind so he can't see how Nick's words have torn through me. "I don't know what pain is? My mom was murdered, my dad tried to commit suicide, and I had to pull the gun out of his mouth. I've got nobody left in the world. I wake up with nightmares every night. And I don't know what *pain* is?"

Nick slowly stands up, holding his hands in the air. He looks at me, and his eyes aren't mocking this time. "Okay, okay," he says, kicking the ground with his shoe. "Sorry. Didn't know."

"Didn't ask," I snap.

We walk on, but he doesn't tease me this time by running ahead. He waits for me, and we walk together, although several feet apart.

The darkness falls quickly. One moment there are streaks of light across the sky, and the next, the dark is so deep that only the thick slice of moon penetrates the black sky. The desolate flatland has shifted into a sparse forest, the trees getting denser with every step, so walking in the dark is even more difficult. My legs are pulsing with pain, and I can hear howling in the distance.

"What's that?" I ask, unable to keep the terror out of my voice.

"Feral dogs," Nick says. "They're everywhere, and a pack of them will rip you to shreds. When my dad was still around, he'd take me on walks after he got off work. He didn't want me to be afraid of them when it came my time to cross the border. He taught me how to scare them away by getting as big as I could, like this." Nick stands up on his tiptoes and stretches his arms over his head. He does look pretty scary. "Never run; you don't want them to chase you."

"You won't let them eat me?" I ask. I'm half kidding, but the other half is very, very serious.

"You wouldn't taste good anyway," he says. "Not enough fat. You're all gristle."

"Gristle?" I ask. *I'm all gristle.* It makes me feel a little tougher, like I'm pulled together out of weeds and spiny thorns.

"Yep, gristle," Nick says, his arm bumping gently into mine. I notice that Nick and I are walking side by side now, and strangely, it feels normal, and kind of comforting.

"Did you ever try to cross the border?" I ask.

"Many times," Nick says. "I learned English at school so I had an easier time than most, but it still didn't work out," he adds. "Besides, I have responsibilities here now."

"Like what?"

"My godfather wants me to run his shipping business. I'm the closest thing he's got to a son, and he wants to keep the business in the family. Besides, since my dad left, my godfather's the closest thing I've got to a father, too."

I scratch at the dirt caked onto my ankles, wondering why Nick sounds like someone dropped a weight on his chest and ordered him to carry it. "Do you want to run his business?"

"Do I want to? I don't know. But it's what I have to do." Nick shrugs. "Don't you ever do anything you don't want to do?"

I think about the million things I have to do to be part of the perfect Divine family. How every day is scripted for me, from Mary being glued to my side, to constantly dieting to please Pierre, to Dad choosing the movies I star in. *Only Mom ever told me my future wasn't written yet—that I got to write it.*

"All the time," I admit. "Sometimes I wish I could just do what I want, be who I want. I feel kind of stuck, like everyone's making my decisions for me." I stop talking, suddenly embarrassed. "Do you ever feel that way?"

"Yeah, I do," Nick says grudgingly, but he looks at me with new respect. "I guess that means we have something in common."

"I guess so." I don't want to admit it, but I feel better.

Nick must feel some of the weight lift off him too, because his eyes don't leave my face for a long time after that.

The moon is a glistening half circle in the sky by the time we reach his cousin's house. It's nothing special, just a small ranch home like on the studio's "Downtrodden American Suburb" set. There's a rickety garage beside the house, with a small speedboat rusting inside of it that looks like it hasn't been used in years. Still, the house seems like a mansion compared to the handful of deserted lean-tos we've passed on the way here.

Nick's cousin isn't home yet, but the door is unlocked, so Nick lets us into the house. There's not much furniture, just an orange couch in the bedroom and a wooden table with four mismatched chairs in the kitchen.

"Take a seat," he says, pulling a pot out from under the sink and filling it with water.

I drop into a chair and lay my head down on the kitchen table while Nick takes two tortillas and a hunk of white cheese out of the refrigerator. He tosses them in a pan on the stove, and the smell of burning cheese twists my stomach in knots. I've never been this hungry before (except for all-night shoots for *Zombie Killer*, but then I had a nutritional regimen and a personal dietician), and I don't like it.

"Local specialty, no crickets," Nick says as he places a tortilla stuffed with cheese in front of me, and puts a glass of boiled water beside it. "You'll love it."

Love it? When did I last love food? It's been years since I've thought about anything other than the calorie count.

I grab the glass of water with both hands and drink it in one big gulp. "My ex-boyfriend never would have let me eat this," I admit. "It has too many calories."

"Sounds like a jerk," Nick says.

"You don't know the half of it." It's embarrassing to talk about, but for some reason, I do. "My boyfriend dumped me for my best friend. In front of a lot of people."

"Ouch."

"Yeah. I hate him."

Nick's eyes narrow into little slits. "Want me to kill him for you?"

Yes. Absolutely. I shake my head. Nick pushes away his empty plate and inches nearer to me, so close I can almost feel the heat on his skin.

With his body so close to mine, I'm so nervous I'm shaking. "What about you?" I ask, stumbling over my words. "When did you . . . um . . . graduate?" *I sound like an idiot.*

"Last year," Nick says. "From an American high school in Mexico City."

"Why an American school?"

"My godfather sent me there when I was thirteen." Nick rolls his eyes. "He said I needed to learn English to run his company." He shakes his head in disgust. "Lot of good it's done me. Now I work as a courier for my godfather's company, just shuttling boxes around. But I owe him," he adds.

"For what?"

"He paid for my education from prison," Nick says. "*Fifteen years* for tax evasion." He shakes his head in disgust. "Just to scare people into paying their taxes. 'But that's the government for you,' my mom used to say."

"Used to?"

Nick looks away, suddenly too busy clearing our dishes to answer.

"Nick? What do you mean by 'used to'?"

Shaking his head, Nick turns the sink handle and drops our dishes into the basin, the ceramic clattering together before sinking into the water completely.

"You don't have to tell me." *Did I say something wrong, or does he not want to talk to me?*

"You're just not at all what I would expect," Nick says, turning around to look at me.

What? Instantly pissed off, I sit back and cross my arms over my chest. "What do you mean by 'expect'?"

Nick blushes. "From an American lost in the wilderness with only a stranger to keep her company."

Good answer. "Are you still a stranger then?"

But as his lips curl into a grin, I realize that he *is* still a stranger. And as much as I want to tell him the truth about me, I can't. I've probably told him too much already. If he were to tell anybody who I am, I'd risk both our lives. Besides, I kind of like being anonymous. All my life, people have liked me because I'm famous, because I'm a Divine. But I think Nick's even beginning to like me—for myself.

Chapter Nine

I SWEAR I'VE BEEN ASLEEP on the couch for only two minutes when I jolt awake, the house drenched in sunshine. Dust motes swim through the air, floating from sunbeam to sunbeam. I'm wrapped in a rainbow-patterned blanket, and Nick's pulled a wool hat over my head.

When I walk into the kitchen, Nick's wearing his white undershirt with just a towel wrapped around his waist, and his hair is dripping wet and curling into damp ringlets on his forehead. *Wow.*

It hits me that I didn't lie awake last night, terrified of falling asleep to bad dreams; I just lay down and went to sleep, listening to Nick's steady breathing.

"So where's your cousin?" I ask with a slight smile.

"He never came home," Nick says, and the half smile dies on my face. "Let's wait a bit. He's gotta come home before work," he continues, handing me a glass of boiled water. "If you wanna take a shower, it's in there."

I down the tall glass of warm water and step into the small, tidy bathroom. It's the complete opposite of Pierre's bathroom, which is stuffed with expensive colognes and hair gel, but then again, Pierre has more beauty products than I do. *It's our job to look good,* Pierre would say, showing off his bags of free swag he got from Etv! parties. *We're in the biz-ness.* Yeah, right. *The business of being a scumbag.* I'm inventing ways to make Pierre miserable, starting with putting quick-acting hair remover in his shampoo bottles, when I hear a crash from the kitchen.

"Nick?" I call timidly. "Are you okay?" I open the door, and bright yellow egg yolk soaks into the spaces between my toes. *What's going on?*

"Stay there," Nick says. He's dressed now and crouched on the floor, surrounded by a yellow pool of yolk and broken eggshells. The ragged edges of the eggs look sharp, like broken glass.

"What happened?"

"Shut the door and lock it," he whispers. "Someone's here."

What does he mean, someone's here? Isn't that what we're waiting for? For his cousin to arrive?

"Go in the bathroom and lock the door," Nick says again, and it slowly sinks in: *The man from the church. He's found me.*

My feet are iron weights on my useless legs. "Come with me."

Nick glances over his shoulder, and then crawls across the kitchen floor to the bathroom, his knees dragging in the broken eggshells. "We'll go out the window," he says, locking the door behind him. He hoists the window up, then grabs my shoes and drops them out. "When I say it's clear, follow me." Before I can ask him anything more, he shimmies out the window. "Clear."

Someone bangs on the bathroom door. I climb out behind Nick, my feet sticky with egg yolk, and he helps me down onto the bed of pine needles.

"Ouch!"

Nick claps his hand over my mouth to stifle my cry. As I pull my shoes on, I hear the dry crackle of wood splintering. *He's breaking down the door.*

"Follow me," Nick says, pulling me to my feet. I wince as dry needles crack beneath my shoes. "This way." He grabs my hand and we run into the safety of the forest.

I feel like we've run for miles, my hand tight in his, before Nick finally slows down. We're in the thickest woods I've ever seen. Vines wide as snakes climb from tree to tree, making a woven forest canopy that blocks out the sky. A stream winds through the few drops of light that are filtering through the trees.

I lean over, my hands on my knees, trying to get my breath back. With each inhalation, my nose is filled with the rich scent of loamy soil. My feet are blistering in my shoes now, and the sticky egg yolk has congealed between my toes. *Yuck.* "Who was that?" I ask, my side splitting with pain.

"I don't know. He looked like a cop, and down here, cops shoot first and ask questions later," Nick says. "But whoever he is, he can't find us out here, if we stay off the road. This forest is hundreds of miles wide. And if we head straight uphill, we can get to Rosales tomorrow."

Looking around, I realize Nick's right that nobody can find us here. We're in the middle of nowhere. The only sign of civilization is a little wooden shack with a tin roof, a radio antennae sticking out of the top. The door is ajar, the scratchy sound of mariachi music leaking out of it. Inside, a woman glances up at us, her head still lowered over a small pile of dead fish. She slices into the bright red belly of a fish, never taking her eyes off us.

"Who is she?" I ask.

"She's a Zapotec. One of the indigenous tribes that ruled Mexico before the Spanish arrived. My godfather calls them *perros*, dogs," Nick says, shaking his head. "But they're harmless."

Outside the door, a small boy, wearing only a black cowboy hat and a red Coca-Cola T-shirt hanging down to his knees, reaches inside a tin barrel of water as tall as he is. With two fingers, he pulls out a giant bullfrog by the feet, its big mouth puffing out in protest.

With the boy's oversized cowboy hat, he reminds me of old pictures of Dad, when he was a child actor in Western shoot-'em-ups. Dad says he got his craving for authenticity then, because the Indians were portrayed as bloodthirsty savages, but the cowboys were the ones who really did the killing. *Tell the truth*, Dad always says, *and the audience believes.*

"We should keep going," Nick says. He yawns, stretching his arms above his head, and his jersey lifts off his muscular back. In the middle of his lower back is the tattoo of a skeleton in a wedding gown. She's holding a scale in her hands, and her eye sockets are empty, but she has a ghastly smile on her face.

It's not like tattoos are new to me. Everyone in L.A. has a tattoo, but they're usually some ancient symbol meaning eternal happiness or world peace, not something out of a horror flick. "What is it?" I ask, trying to hide my shock. I mean, I've kinda had a tattoo too. Last year I wore a heart sticker on my lower back for the whole summer, and by August, I had a bright white heart on my skin. Pierre called it a tramp stamp. *But at least mine was a heart!*

"Santa Muerte," Nick says. "When my godfather was in

prison, I got it to show solidarity with him."

A shriek of delight suddenly pierces the air. On the other side of the stream, the boy in the black cowboy hat dashes away from his sister's swinging arms, running straight toward us. But when the boy sees us, he grinds to a halt. Dust swirls around his feet as he stares at us, unblinking, a terrified look on his face.

Then the boy starts yelling a word I can't understand, over and over. It sounds like it's coming from deep down in his throat. Each scream is like ripping a hair out by its root, and I clap my hands over my ears so that I can't hear it again. The woman glares at us, her hand tightening around her sharp, bloody knife.

With the boy still bellowing, Nick yanks his shirt down over his back and grabs my hand. He hikes straight uphill, away from the village, his face filled with rage.

"What did that boy say?" I ask. "And why was that woman so angry?" *Or scared. She was definitely scared.* I stamp my feet, dust spitting up around my shoes. "What are you so mad about?"

"Why am I mad?" Nick stops beside a fallen tree trunk, where colonies of squirmy black insects are crawling around the pile of branches. He turns to me, and the anger drops off his face. His smile grows lean, mischievous. "Because he called you the White Devil."

My mouth falls open in surprise. "The White Devil?"

"He's just ignorant," Nick says. "Don't worry about it."

Don't worry about it? A woman with a bloody weapon thinks I'm a demon and I'm not supposed to worry about it?

"But we'd better get going, devil girl, if you want to find food before nightfall."

"Find? Like look under rocks? Or do you know of a taco stand around here?"

Nick grins, then leans over and wipes a bead of sweat off my face. My skin tingles where he touches it, and I feel my body being drawn toward his. *Hello? This is Nick, who calls me a spoiled princess and fools me into eating crickets.* But my head is dizzy with the closeness of him, and every cell in my body is pulling me toward him. Then he's leaning in too, the space between our lips vibrating with heat. *He's going to kiss me.*

Nick pulls away suddenly, his eyes blazing. "Um . . . I'll take care of it," he says, dropping his gaze to the ground. He turns and walks into the woods.

As soon as I'm alone, my fear comes back, rolling over me in waves. The memory of that man's gravelly voice in the church makes me shiver under my layers of sweat. *Did he follow me to Nick's cousin's house? What would've happened if Nick weren't there to protect me? Nick's right: I couldn't take care of myself if it punched me in the face.* I fight the urge to curl up on the ground and cry. The only thing that stops me is the silence. It's so large that Nick would hear me going totally fetal in an instant, because I can hear every sound for miles around. And then I hear something that makes my skin crawl:

The crunch of footsteps behind me.

I'm too terrified to look back, so I make myself a deal: count to ten, and then do it. By the time I get to five, all I can imagine is someone blowing my head off from behind, so I do it: I look back.

It's not a killer.

It's the boy.

Under the curved brim of his cowboy hat, he's staring into the woods, focused on the place where Nick walked into the trees. The boy says something then, his voice anxious. I can't understand anything, but he repeats the same word as before: White Devil.

I'm starting to get insulted. *Why did he chase me down if he thinks I'm the White Devil?* "Speak English?" I ask.

The boy shakes his head, and then starts speaking rapidly in his language. I can't understand a word of it. It doesn't sound like Spanish, not that I'd understand that either. He crouches down, smoothes out the ground in front of us, and draws something in the dirt with his index finger.

"A stick?" I say as a long, wavy rectangle finds its way out of the dirt. He shakes his head and draws a line coming out of it.

"A lizard?" He shakes his head again, his black cowboy hat falling over his eyes.

I hear Nick's footsteps crunching on the dirt behind us. The little boy pushes his shaking finger into the ground again. He draws a circle coming out of the rectangle and looks at me, willing me to get it. It must have worked, because suddenly, I do:

A gun. He's drawing a gun.

Panic surges through me. *Why would he draw a gun? Did he see that man following us from the house?* I squint into the thick green forest, and a shudder cycles through my body. I feel enemies hiding behind every tree, but besides the squirrel racing across a branch with a nut in his teeth, and Nick walking toward us empty-handed, there's no one out here. *Nobody's following us.*

"What's the kid doing here?" Nick asks.

"I don't know. He followed me."

"He must be hungry."

Facing the little boy, I point to myself, shake my head, and then stuff an imaginary burger into my mouth. "We don't have any food."

The boy looks at Nick, then back at me. He repeats that word again, the one that means I'm the White Devil, and then he jumps up and sprints full speed down the road. We both watch him go, dust spitting up beneath his bare feet.

"Poor kid," I say. "I can't imagine being that hungry."

"I can."

I don't know what to say to that, so I don't say anything. I just stand up and dust off the back of my jeans, hoping Nick notices the effects of my weekly abs and butt workouts. He doesn't. He just points to the boy's drawing in the dirt.

"What's that?"

Since when has a kid's stick drawing been more interesting than my butt?

"I think it's a gun," I say, "but I don't know why he drew it."

"Probably because of this," Nick says, pulling a small black revolver out of the side pocket of his cargo pants.

Chapter Ten

OUR EYES LOCK, AND MY chest burns with fear as if I've just pressed it against a hot stove. *Is Nick going to kill me?* Sweat pops up across my forehead, dripping off my eyebrows and stinging my eyes. *Was he just being nice to lure me into the woods and shoot me?*

"Why do you have a gun?" My voice is quaking so much, I can hardly make out the words. *How could I be foolish enough to trust him? It all seems so absurd now: coincidently meeting on the bus, following him through the woods, him being so protective of me.*

"How'd you think I was going to get us food?" Nick asks. "Beat it with a stick?"

The burn in my chest lets up a little, and I wipe the sweat off my forehead and rub my wet hands on my jeans. "You use it to hunt?"

"And for protection. What else would I use it for?" he asks.

Relief floods through my body, relaxing my muscles and soothing my burning chest. "Why didn't you tell me you had a gun?"

"I didn't want to scare you," he says. "But I guess I did."

"I guess," I say, like it's no big deal, like people pull guns on me every day. *Actually, they do, but it's in a studio and the guns are loaded with blanks.*

"Would you feel better if I took the bullets out?" Nick asks.

He has the bullets in? I nod, not able to get my voice back yet. Doesn't he know he could shoot his private parts off carrying it in his pocket? (It happens, at least in movies.)

Nick takes the bullets out and puts them in his back pocket. Then he smiles, and to my surprise, it's a beautiful, better-than-Hollywood smile. Despite his macho attitude and the gun in his hand, my heart melts a little.

"By the way," he grins. "Nice butt."

By the time we stop again, the sun is setting over the mountains. Billowing clouds of fog soak the tops of the trees, making the entire world glow a deep orange. The air is thick and damp on my bare skin, and it smells moist and new.

The forest floor is a soft orange rug, whispering in the slight breeze. Even the trees look like they're wrapped in orange silk. I've never seen anything like it: it actually looks like the trees are breathing.

"Let's stop here," Nick whispers, stepping into a small clearing and gesturing for me to sit beside him in a patch of grass. "This is a good place to build a fire."

"Why are you whispering?" I ask, my voice booming through the forest.

Suddenly the whole forest floor shifts, lifting in one fluttered movement, like a magic carpet. Then millions of orange wings burst into the air, stripping the trees and fields of color.

For a moment, the world fills with butterflies.

I feel wings flutter against my cheek as thousands of butterflies surround me. I feel like I'm in a remake of *Cinderella* where butterflies have arrived to sew my dress and escort me to the ball.

"Where did they all come from?" I whisper.

"You don't have to whisper anymore." Nick laughs. "They know we're here."

I raise my arms, palms up. In the deepening light my skin looks exactly how photographers airbrush it to be: golden, limber, supple. I hold as still as I can as countless butterflies land on my arms with their soft, tickly feet, covering me from shoulder to wrist.

"I think they like me."

A slow smile creeps over Nick's face. "Smart butterflies," he says, sitting close beside me on the forest floor, his gaze locked on mine. It feels like butterflies have inhabited my chest, beating their wings unbearably fast. "They fly thousands of miles just to rest in this forest every winter," he says.

"Why here?" I ask, noticing how my arms, still extended straight out, are starting to shake. Butterflies are jumping off my quaking skin, joining the circling orange-and-black sky.

"Nobody knows," Nick says. "But when the locals look at them, they see angels."

"What do you see?"

"Something even better," Nick says, looking right at me.

After the butterflies have resettled, covering the forest in rich orange velvet, Nick helps me start a fire. And when I say help, I mean he does the whole thing and gives me credit. *Just the way I like it.* If Pierre was here, he'd pretend he knew how to do it, burn himself, and then make me start the fire. In the end, he'd take all the credit anyway. But not Nick; his praise is so believable I almost think I did it myself.

Once the fire is roaring, Nick extracts his gun from his side pocket and holds it out where I can see it, careful to point it away from me. He's so nervous about scaring me. *How could I ever have doubted him?*

"I'm gonna use my gun now," he warns, "to get us dinner. Unless you want me to head butt a bunny."

"I'd really love to see that," I say, "as long as I'm not the bunny."

We grin at each other before he heads off into the forest to hunt.

Seconds later, I hear a gunshot, and then Nick returns, swinging what looks like a dead squirrel by the tail. I'm so grossed out I can barely speak.

"Did I mention I'm never eating again?" I ask, staring at the squirrel's furry body as Nick skins it with his small pocketknife. I have to look away as he cuts it open and impales it on a stick, and then hangs it over the fire, inches from the flames. "Seriously, *never* again," I repeat.

Despite my protests, within minutes the squirrel is roasting over the fire with bits of its flesh crackling. A few butterflies are swirling in the smoke over the flames, but the rest have settled into the forest, still as ghosts.

"Just try it," Nick says, blowing on a piece of the steaming cooked squirrel hanging from a stick. "One piece won't kill you."

I seriously doubt that. You don't just eat a squirrel and live! "No way."

"Scared?" Nick taunts.

"Okay, gimme that." Aware that I'm going to spend the rest of the night waiting for food poisoning to kill me, I grab the stick from him and bite off a piece of meat. It practically melts in my mouth. "It tastes like chicken," I say through another mouthful.

Nick grins at me, and his smile is almost worth eating rodent intestines. *Almost.*

After we've eaten, we settle back into the darkness of the forest, our shoulders lightly touching in the dark. I'm surprised at how safe I feel, now that I'm really hidden from the world for the first time in my life. Besides Nick, no one knows I'm here. No paparazzi, no police, no magazines looking for their next story. *Not even that horrible man could find me here.* The thought of him sends beads of sweat down my back.

"You look nervous," Nick says. In the firelight, his eyes flicker from dark green to light green, and I feel like I'm being hypnotized, his irises a swinging watch at the end of a long chain. His eyelashes are longer than mine (not fair!), curling up a bit at the ends, and his eyes seem to breathe me in, *all* of me, not just little useful pieces like Pierre's used to do. *But maybe I'm just imagining it.*

"It's just . . . I'm glad you're here," I say, praying he won't laugh at me. "I mean, there must be lots of girls wishing they were in my position."

Hiding from a killer with an armed stranger in Mexico? Am I crazy?

Nick looks at me in surprise. "Not really. I pretty much stay to myself," he says. "I like being alone."

Here's a major difference between us: I can't imagine what's possibly fun about being alone. In fact, I can't think of a time when I was. My life is scheduled out for me, every hour penciled in with journalists, photo shoots, interviews.

"This is the first time I've ever been alone," I say quietly.

Nick pretends to pout. "Am I that bad of company?"

"No, it's actually the opposite," I say, a blush spreading up my cheeks. "I feel like I can tell you anything. I haven't felt this way since—"

"Since when?"

"Since my mom died."

Nick turns and gazes into the fire, as if he's searching in the flames for something to say. "You were really close?" he finally asks.

"She was the only person who ever really knew me," I say softly, remembering the way Mom and I would blurt out the same thing at the same time. Then she'd laugh and say, *You're thinking that?* Like I was the only one thinking it. "It's like . . . she knew what I was going to say before I said it."

I expect Nick to look confused, like Pierre did when I told him, but he's nodding like he understands.

"Without her, I feel so, I don't know, hollow," I say. *Okay, so that was embarrassing. Stop talking!* But I can't, because something beyond my control is pushing the words out of my mouth. "I guess I'm just . . ." I bite my lower lip to stop talking, but the words come rolling out, stinging and raw in the air between us. "I'm just afraid I'll never feel happy again."

Nick is silent for a moment. I'm expecting all the usual things: She'd Want You to Be Happy, Life Goes On, Keep Your Head Up. But Nick gives me something I'd never expect: "I'm afraid of the same thing."

I'm shocked that Nick's afraid of anything. He carries a gun, and he can skin a squirrel with a pocketknife. What could he possibly be afraid of?

"You are?"

He nods. "I was really close to my mom too. It was just the two of us for so long."

"What happened to your dad?"

"He just handed me and Mom off to my godfather, and left. He didn't love me enough to stick around, I guess." Nick shrugs. "And if my own father couldn't love me . . ." Nick picks up a piece of gnarled wood and feeds it to the fire's hungry mouth. As the flames devour it, his voice drops to a barely audible level. "Then why would anyone else?"

"I'm sure, if your dad saw you now, he'd love you." *If he saw what I see*, I want to add.

I can barely hear Nick's voice when he speaks again. "Not after what I did to my mom."

"It can't be that bad," I insist, scooting a little closer to him.

"It is." He hesitates for a long time. I know he doesn't want to talk about it, but for some reason, I need to hear.

"What happened?"

"I left her to die," Nick says.

"You *what?*"

"I convinced Mom to cross *la frontera* with me. She didn't want to, but I thought there had to be a better life for us there, where we made our own money, and we didn't have to depend on my godfather." Nick adds another piece of dry wood to the fire. "But then—when we were crossing the desert in the middle of the night, a car drove up. I thought it was Immigration, so I started to run."

"Didn't she run too?"

"I thought she was with me, but then I heard a shot. Someone fell, and I just knew. I knew it was Mom."

"What did you do?"

"I kept running," Nick says, his voice so choked up he can barely get the words out. "I was such a coward. And when I finally went back, she was dead."

I want to tell him it's going to be okay, but it will never be okay, for either of us. Beside me, Nick's tears are quiet, like drops of water at the bottom of a well. I can feel the hole inside of him—it's as big as mine.

We sit in silence for a long time after that, until the fire has simmered down to a layer of muted red and the pops of the dying branches poke holes in the empty space inside of me.

"It's not your fault," I whisper. Each word reverberates inside my body, like someone beating on a hollowed-out stick.

"It *is* my fault," Nick says. "I'm the one who wanted to cross the border. I'm the one who ran away and left her to die."

"You can't blame yourself," I insist, thinking of the hours Mary's spent trying to convince me of the exact same thing. And it's true: Nick may have led his mom across the border, but he didn't kill her; and despite all the guilt I've put on myself, despite the note Mom got before she was kidnapped, the one that said, "I'm coming for the girl," I wasn't the person who killed my mom. *It's not my fault. I have to stop blaming myself.*

"I just wish," Nick continues, "I wish I had been shot instead."

"Don't say that!" I exclaim, and I desperately need him to believe me, to not blame himself, so I can stop feeling all this guilt too. "You couldn't have known what would happen."

"Logically, I know that. But inside . . ." Nick takes a deep breath. His chest rattles as he breathes it out. "You wouldn't understand."

"But I *do* understand. When my mom died, I blamed myself, too," I blurt out, "but it wasn't my fault." I take a deep breath to keep my voice from shaking. "And it wasn't your fault either." I stare into the dying fire, thinking about how our moms' deaths happened *to* us, but not *because* of us. *It wasn't our fault.*

Nick slides his arm around me and draws me closer. "I miss my mom every day."

"Me too."

All of a sudden, the dark isn't so dark. I nestle against Nick's shoulder, letting silence and the crackling of the fire fill me with his words. I feel like there's a cut straight through his soul, and I'm looking into it.

I see your soul, I want to say, but I bite my tongue, and hope he sees mine.

My own scream wakes me. I sit straight up, my skin itching with fear.

"What's wrong?" Nick asks, sitting up beside me.

It's another nightmare. I'm in the black box again, something pressing into me from all sides, but I don't feel guilty this time, I just feel scared.

"Are you okay?" Nick searches my face for an answer, but I can't bring myself to speak. I shake my head, and as if the tears were lodged in there, they shake out and pour down my cheeks.

Nick strokes the tears off my face, and I'm embarrassed, but I can't stop crying.

I never cry in front of anyone! Even at Mom's funeral I didn't shed a single tear for the cameras. But this time, it's like the floodgates opened, and my fear and sadness and shame are pouring out all over him.

But Nick doesn't seem to mind. He takes me in his arms and rocks me, back and forth, more gently than I ever thought possible. I don't want to speak, to ruin the moment. And then I think: *This is the most intimate moment I've ever had.* So I let him hold me and rock me and rub my back. Neither of us says a word. Then the impossible happens: I drift back off to sleep, somehow comforted in Nick's arms.

Chapter Eleven

I WAKE THE NEXT MORNING still wrapped in Nick's arms. The world is unbearably bright, and it smells like pine needles and damp soil. I bury my head in his chest, wanting to stay there forever. But nature has other ideas. I wait until pain fills my bladder, wanting every last moment with Nick, then I stand up and hobble deeper into the woods to find a place to pee.

The woods aren't so scary this morning. They're dressed in the orange-and-black wings of monarchs. There's a flowering meadow to my left, and when I glance to my right, I'm surprised to see that we are less than fifty feet from the windy dirt road. *We were supposed to stay off the road, but we must have crossed it last night in the dark.*

After I find a place to pee, I stand up and head back toward Nick, amazed at how the ground is a fluttering orange carpet, its smooth surface broken only by a small mound at the end of the clearing. *A bundle of firewood?* I imagine the pride lighting up Nick's face when I return, cradling an armful of wood for our morning fire.

As I walk, butterflies lift into the air and swirl around my legs, their wings tickling my skin. I feel something growing inside of me, a small flame of happiness that I haven't felt since Mom died. I want to cup my hands around it, to protect this tiny feeling of joy flickering inside of me, warming the ice that's frozen across my heart. I think of Nick's arms, his smile, his strong chest pressed against my back . . .

When I reach the mound at the end of the clearing, it's layered with butterflies. There's a sweet smell that I can't place. I reach down to grab the wood, and the butterflies spring off it, leaving something exposed in the sunshine: a body.

My scream echoes through the forest, bouncing off trees and scaring the whole forest to life. Orange wings rain down on me, beating against me like a heavy snow. Birds call in shrieking high voices. I hear Nick yell "Ines!" and his footsteps charging toward me. All this is happening in slow motion, as if from very far away, because I can't do anything but look at him: the dark suit, pale skin, and two giant orange butterflies resting on his eyelids.

A physical pain surges in my chest, rolling up my throat, into the back of my mouth . . . I vomit in the bushes. I crouch over and try to hide myself behind a tree. The bitter taste of vomit coats the back of my tongue.

Nick skids to a stop when he reaches me, the branches breaking under his weight like snapping bones. "That's him!" he exclaims. "The man at my cousin's house!"

The world speeds up to its normal pace, and I realize I'm trembling from head to toe. "Are you sure?" My voice is frantic, and I have to work to keep it steady.

Nick nods. "Are you okay?"

Do I look okay? Is anything about this situation okay? I wipe off my mouth and crawl out from behind the tree, embarrassment pushing heat into my cheeks. "What should we do?" I ask, turning my head away in case my breath smells rotten.

"Let's get out of here. Somebody didn't want him found, and if they know we found him . . ." Nick says. "I don't know what will happen. But it has nothing to do with us."

It has nothing to do with you. And everything to do with me. I suck on my front teeth, trying to swallow back the taste of vomit in my mouth. *And it's not just you that I'm putting in danger. What if Dad's dead in the middle of nowhere, thanks to me? What if they tortured him to find out where I am, and when he wouldn't give me up, they killed him?*

I push back the thought and force myself to look at the dead man: the tailored pants, the crisp suit jacket, the perfectly knotted tie . . . I stop just below the face. I can't look at it, not with those orange butterflies resting over his dead eyes.

"We've gotta get out of here now," Nick says.

"Shouldn't we do something to—"

"Did you hear that?" Nick interrupts me, his voice a thick whisper.

"I didn't hear anything," I say, looking at the dead man's lips. I'm waiting for them to move, to form the words *help me*. I remember Dad on the day Mom was killed: how he cried out to her when I kneeled beside him, and how behind him, the TV alternated between images of Mom's knifed back and that horrible building in an endless loop. I turned off the TV and swore I'd never see those images again. *But I did—when it was my turn to die.*

"That," Nick says again, and I hear it this time: a car engine rattling up the road. "I'll find out who it is." He pulls his gun from his pocket and drops two bullets in the chamber. "Stay here. If I'm not back in two minutes, run."

"You're gonna leave me here?" *Definitely a bad idea.* The last time I was alone, my bag was stolen and I would have died on the roadside if it weren't for Nick. I grab his hand

and squeeze as hard as I can. "Please don't go."

"I'll be right back. You can see me from here." Nick points to the dusty mountain road not far from the clearing, a short enough distance to run to if I need him. He strokes the back of his hand softly across my cheek. "He can't hurt you. He's dead."

Nick's wrong about that. The dead can hurt you. Much worse than the living.

"I'll be right back, okay?" Nick gives me a reassuring smile and walks through the trees, looking back every few steps to make sure I'm okay.

"Okay," I whisper. But I'm not okay. If I were okay, I wouldn't be sitting by a dead body in the middle of the woods in Mexico, waiting for someone to find me and kill me. But at least the body hasn't come back to life and dragged me into his grave—yet.

I inch a little closer, wondering who he is, what he's doing out here, and most importantly, if he was looking for me.

A morbid fascination creeps over me. Despite the thin red line across his throat where somebody sliced the life out of him, he looks like he could be sleeping. I lean a little closer to the man, my heart pounding. Beneath me, a stick snaps, loud as a gunshot.

I jump, and the butterflies scatter off the man's face. His eyes are open in terror, but it's not the look that scares me. It's the colors.

One brown eye. One blue.

It's the FBI agent Mary hit with the limo.

I bite down on my bottom lip so I don't scream aloud, and sink backward, vomit rising in my throat again. I picture him flipping over the roof, the way his mouth opened and closed silently behind the thick glass. *He was following me this whole time.*

It feels like a hundred years ago that I was huddled in my limo, frozen under his gun's black eye. *Who killed him?* A wave of shock ripples through me, paralyzing me with fear. *Are they going to kill me, too?*

The roar of an engine startles me out of my thoughts. I hear Nick shouting something in Spanish and brakes squealing to a stop. I glance through the trees to the road, where Nick's standing with his back to me. *I have to know why he was following me. If I don't find out now, I'll never know.*

Hoping Nick doesn't turn around, I push my fingers into the FBI agent's shirt pockets. *Empty. There's got to be something here. A business card, a cell phone, anything to tell me why he was following me.* I rifle through his pants pockets, and then turn to his suit jacket. *I can't believe I'm doing this. Is stealing from the FBI a federal crime?*

From the inside left pocket of his suit jacket, I pull out his FBI badge. *Agent Patterson. Temporary replacement ID.*

I shove his badge back into his jacket, and then dig into

his other inside pocket. My fingers catch on a small white envelope. *Bingo.* I open the envelope and shake out the contents. A ragged napkin falls onto his dead chest, and a folded piece of paper lands in the grass by my feet. I pick the napkin up with my fingertips and inspect it quickly. On the back is a hastily scribbled set of numbers:

12.03.60.6.

Are these lotto numbers? Why would he be playing lotto at a time like this? Slowly the numbers fall into place: *They're my bus numbers from L.A. and Tijuana.* I picture Mary's note, the one she told me to destroy: *Buy a cash ticket for the 1203 bus to Tijuana, then transfer to the 606 bus to Rosales.* I would have walked right into his hands if the bus hadn't broken down. *He knew everything. What would he have done to me if he'd caught me?*

On the road, the car engine shuts off, and silence crawls over the forest.

Focus. I force my hand to pick up the paper off the ground and unfold it. It's a picture of me. I'm standing with Mary, looking straight into the camera. The edges are torn and wrinkled, as if it's been passed through many hands. *How many people want me dead? And why?*

As I quickly stuff the envelope back into the agent's jacket pocket, I hear footsteps inches behind me. My body relaxes. *Nick's back. He'll know what to do.*

"Nick, I was just looking for—"

"*¿Quién?*"

That isn't Nick's voice. That voice reminds me of urine and churches and looming black shadows. My mouth goes dry, and my tongue scrapes against my chapped lips. And when I turn around, it isn't Nick.

It isn't Nick at all.

Chapter Twelve

THE MAN STANDING IN FRONT of me hardly looks human. He's huge, as big as a tree. A line of rough stitches curves from his forehead to his chin, like someone carved him up and sewed him back together. Gray snakes are tattooed on his face, slithering down his neck, onto his gigantic biceps and gnarly hands.

My whole body cramps with terror, and a lump the size of a fist lodges in my throat. I glance behind me, wondering if I can make it farther into the forest before he reaches me. But before I can move an inch, the man grabs my chin with his bony fingers, his knuckles grinding into my cheekbones as he forces me to look at him.

"Vivian," he growls.

I back away slowly, snapping twigs beneath my feet, until his arm is completely stretched out, his bony hand still wrapped around my chin. "Where's Nick?" I whimper.

He grabs my wrist with his other hand and clenches down on my arm until it feels like my bones will break. I'm so focused on the searing pain in my arm that I hardly notice that he's pulling me through the forest like a piece of dead firewood, my feet barely touching the ground.

"Nick!" I scream. "Help!"

But when we break through the trees, there's nobody on the road.

"What did you do to Nick?"

The man slides his fingertip across his burly neck. *Please tell me he didn't cut Nick's throat.*

"NICK!" I scream at the top of my lungs.

The man flings open the passenger door and shoves me in. Under my thick layer of fear, I feel anger rush through the cracks. *What if Nick needs me?*

Imagining Nick's bloody body, a fire sparks in the base of my stomach. *He could be lying half-dead in the bushes, bleeding to death!* Anger explodes inside me and I throw myself against the door, but it's locked from the outside. *Try the window.* I grab the handle, and I've rolled the window down an inch when the driver's door is wrenched open and the man is sitting beside me, his horrible face only inches from mine.

* * *

We fly up the mountain road, dust coating the car in a thick skin. Biting my lip to keep from crying, I watch the ground fly by, gauging if it would kill me to jump.

I've done it before. I jumped out of a moving car for a stunt in *Zombie Killer*. Dad taught me to push my chin into my chest and curl my body into a ball when I jumped. *Make it authentic*, Dad said, and it worked. When I hit the padded floor, it didn't hurt at all. Of course, the car was going only five miles per hour through a fully padded studio. I glance back at the road. *But even if I could get the window down in time to jump out, hitting pure gravel at sixty miles per hour? Not good odds.*

I reach up and put on my seat belt. *At least I won't go through the windshield—if he doesn't kill me first.* "Who sent you?" I ask, my voice quivering so much I can barely make out the words. The man obviously can't work on his own. He wouldn't have made it out of the circus without someone unlocking the cage.

He grunts, then pulls a plastic-wrapped cigar out of his front pocket, rips the plastic off with his teeth, and gnaws off the end. Pieces of brown paper stick to his teeth and lips.

"Please tell me," I whisper, dropping my voice to the most soothing tone I know. *Maybe I can talk him into letting me go. If I just give him the right incentive . . .*

Snatching a lighter off the dashboard, he lights his cigar

and sucks it until the tip glows like the end of a sparkler.

"Just tell me what you did to Nick," I beg. His mouth tightens into a sharp line and he grips the steering wheel tighter with his huge, tattooed hands. *He's listening. Keep talking.* I take a deep breath, getting ready for my big speech. *This is where the heroine talks the villain out of killing her.* I'll explain how he can have a better life than this, that he'll find somebody to love him, that he can get an honest job (maybe in the circus), how with that face, he'd be a great character actor.

"You don't have to do this," I say quietly. "I can help you. I'll take you back to Hollywood with me. My agent can get you a role in a movie. We could even get you plastic surgery—"

A voice erupts right above my head, and I jump so high I hit the ceiling, almost smacking my temple on the CB radio poking out of the rearview mirror. *"Scars!"* the voice orders over the CB. *"Atención!"*

"Scars?" I repeat, and the tattooed man glares at me in response. *So his name is Scars? You've got to be kidding me. Are we in the movie* The Godfather *or something?*

"*Silencio,*" Scars says to me as he takes the CB radio out of the front visor. He pushes a red button and lowers his lips to it, one side of his snake-infested face twitching with nerves. *Who on earth could make this man nervous?* "¿*Sí, señor?*" he asks.

"*Tráigala a la casa,*" the voice orders. "¿*Comprende, Scars?*"

"*Comprendo,*" Scars repeats. He flies around a switchback

on the mountain road, and a mix of motion sickness and stark terror makes me focus on the floor. By my feet, there's a folded suit, faded green like a soldier's uniform.

"Are you in the military?" I ask.

"*¿En los militares?*" Scars inhales sharply on his cigar, and his cheeks puff out with smoke. Then coughing erupts from his lips, and smoke billows out in every direction. The cigar shoots out of his mouth and hits the floor. I stare at the lit cigar for a second, burning into the carpet by his foot. *This is my chance.*

In one movement, I grab the burning cigar and shove it into his leg. He howls, wrenching the wheel to the side. We skid off the road, and there's this moment that stretches on and on, where all is silent, and we're slowly careening toward the earth, before the car flips. Then glass shatters around me, and I can't hear my screams over the screech of steel crushing; the ground and sky are switching places, the world breaking into pieces. We flip again. And again.

When it stops, I'm folded into the ceiling. Every muscle in my body hurts. I hear Scars groaning beside me. He's trapped behind the steering wheel, bleeding from the forehead. There's a nasty hole in his leg, the skin already bubbling up around it. He pounds the steering wheel with his fist, and the smell of his burned skin mixes with thick smoke. *The cigar must still be burning.*

I pop off my seat belt, drop to the floor, and kick the door open. Coughing tears from my throat as I breathe in the smoke pouring from the engine. *It's not the cigar: the engine's on fire.*

"Vivian!" Scars screeches, letting out a horrible, wounded animal sound. He grabs my hair, and I whip around and bite his hand as hard as I can. He screams, letting go of my hair. I climb out of the car and scramble up the rocky hillside.

Without the shade of the forest, sun pounds down on the rocks, heating them like the inside of a dry sauna. My fingers burn from grabbing them, and my knees feel like they're bleeding from scrambling over their searing edges. Behind me, Scars's angry voice races up the rocks, grabbing at my heels as I sprint up the mountain.

The *boom* of the explosion stops me in my tracks. The vile stench of gasoline fills the air and smoke climbs up the sky with its grasping paws. The burst of heat rolling over me singes my skin.

Nobody could live through an explosion like that. Even so, for a long time after his voice dies and the smoke settles, I keep running. Scrambling. Crawling. I don't stop running until my side pulses with pain, until rocks have ripped through my jeans and torn most of the skin from my knees.

Chapter Thirteen

I'VE BEEN HIKING UPHILL A couple of hours now, away from Scars and (hopefully) toward Rosales. But my head is aching, and it turns out that hiking isn't anything like the Outdoor Channel says it is.

There aren't any spectacular vistas to look off into the horizon and I haven't seen any perfectly placed boulders or pretty wildflowers. There are just crabby bushes that scratch my ankles when I walk past them, scary moving bodies under rocks, boulders that slide when I step on them. I'm grimy and my legs hurt and sweat drips into my mouth, and my jeans are so hot I want to tear them off my body, but they're stuck to me like a layer of skin.

See that mountain? I hear Nick say. *Rosales is at the very top.* I force myself to keep climbing rock over rock, trying not to stare into the late-morning sun. *If Nick's dead, it's my fault.* Guilt slides over me, sticky and wet as tar. *Don't think about it or you'll die right here, alone, on this mountainside.*

I've slowed my walk to almost a crawl when I reach a dirt road. The road is empty and silent, like no one's driven on it in years. The only car in sight is a yellow truck, lying fifty feet down the steep embankment. The front teeters precariously over the brink, a drop of hundreds of feet. *That's the mariachi band's truck.*

I step off the road and walk down the steep hill toward it. Even though a cool wind is picking up, I feel hotter than ever. Up close, the blue tarp is pocked with bullet holes. The windshield is crushed in, and the driver's seat is wet with a dark stain.

What happened to the little girl? The mariachi band? Is it my fault? I'm staggering backward, my knees shaking uncontrollably, when I hear a wounded crying. Even though every bone in my body doesn't want to do it, I follow the sound to the truck bed. The lamb is in there, wrapped in a tight ball.

"Honey?"

Bleating a low cry, Honey rises to his shaky legs and pulls himself down the truck bed toward me. When he gets to the open gate, he falls off the side and smashes into the ground. *Walk away, Vivian. You can't save him.* I slowly back up, and Honey climbs to his feet and tries to follow me, but his legs are shaking, and he crumples face-first into the dirt. *I can't just leave him here to die.*

I slowly lower my hands to the ground. "Please don't bite me," I say as I wrap my hands under his belly and lift him up. He cradles his head against my chest as I cross the road and walk up into the mountains. I don't look back.

By now my legs are so tired I'm stumbling. I've put Honey down only once so he could drink water from a stream, and my arms ache from wrist to shoulder from carrying him. Even counting all-night film shoots, I don't think I've ever been this exhausted, but my mind is still wide awake. *I'll reach Rosales soon. Roberto will take me to the safe house, and we'll look for Nick. I have to find him.* And then, for the thousandth time, my mind tortures me with how much I wish Nick were still here, but more than anything, how I wish I could call Mom, and have her tell me how everything will be okay, and that I have a whole story left to write. But here on the deserted mountainside, it feels like my story's ending. *It's a story with a tragic ending, one where the heroine starves to death on the side of a mountain, all alone, with only a lamb to keep her company.*

I wonder if Pierre misses me, and if Dad is frantically searching for me, or if he hasn't even noticed I'm gone. I wonder what happened to the girl I was before Mom died, and if I'll ever get her back. Even though it's only been six months, I can hardly remember who that girl was.

How can so much change in so little time? My head starts to feel heavy, and my legs stick like magnets to the ground. *I can't go on. I'm too tired.* Once again, I wish I were the person Mom thought I was: strong, capable of anything. *I can't even build a fire or find food to save my life.* I realize that Nick was right about me: I'm just a spoiled princess who needs someone else to save her. *And that's all I'll ever be.*

I'm not paying attention to where I'm going anymore, just up, up, up. But as I come over another small hill, I'm startled back to reality by two mangy dogs, eating a long, furry carcass. *The feral dogs are what you really have to watch out for,* I remember Nick saying. *They're everywhere, and a pack of them will rip you to shreds.* Stifling tears, I back up as slowly as I can, nestling Honey tightly to me. *I wish Nick were here. He'd know what to do.* I try to picture the beach, my favorite café, anything—but it's no use. I keep seeing myself being eaten by hungry animals. *I'm going to die all alone out here, torn to pieces by wild beasts.*

Suddenly Honey thrashes in my arms, and then he starts squealing the highest pitched squeal I've ever heard. The dogs look up from the bloody carcass, and as I slowly stumble backward, they crouch down and stalk toward me, growling. I retreat until my back is against a jagged cliff wall, Honey squealing louder and louder every second, and I can't stop thinking that years from now, someone will find my leg bone or elbow joint, and DNA will prove it was me. *The missing child star?* they'll say. *Vivian who?*

The boom of a shotgun rattles through the cliff behind me, and the dogs take off running. Then someone jumps onto the ground in front of me, trapping me against the cliff. News headlines of people being tortured to death fill my mind: *Vivian Divine was found with her fingernails pulled out. Body intact, head a mile away.*

For a moment there is only silence as she stares at me. Then tears gather in the folds of her gigantic black eyes, and her lips form a word I've never heard before. "Paloma?" she asks, and then, as if she's just seen me, she draws back, her face solid as petrified wood. "No," she says quietly to herself.

I shake my head, wishing I were whoever she thought I was. *She's gonna leave now. I'm gonna die at the jaws of rabid beasts.* But she doesn't leave. Her face cracks in pain, and I see the wrong girl reflected in her eyes. She takes Honey, and then pulls me up and wraps me tenderly in her arms. I break into loud, gasping tears, thankful she didn't leave me to get torn to shreds by wild dogs. The woman cradles my face against her shoulder.

"*Ay dios,*" she sighs.

I'm numb all over. She puts her arm around me and leads me up the rocky hillside.

Chapter Fourteen

THE SUN IS ALMOST SETTING over the mountain when we reach the woman's house. The smell of ammonia smothers me and chickens shriek, loud enough to make my skin crawl.

"*No tengas miedo,*" the woman says, leading me away from the chickens to a small concrete house. She points to a rusted folding chair just outside the door, and I sit down gratefully as she places Honey back in my arms. He baas at me, and I kiss the top of his head, then rub my lips against the back of my hand, wondering what diseases I just contracted from his dirty fur.

"*¿Hablas inglés?*" the woman asks me.

I nod, and then I hear the angels sing. They sound like this:

"I speak English," she says, and although her Mexican accent is thick, and the last word sounds like Engl*eesh*, I can understand her just fine.

A smile breaks over my face. "Where did you learn English?"

"My sister taught me."

"Is she here?"

"She's dead." She disappears into the house, returning quickly with a bowl of leaves and a bottle of rubbing alcohol. "We need to clean those wounds before they get infected," she says. "Just hold your breath." Before I can ask why, she rubs alcohol on my skinned knees poking out of my jeans, and they burn like they're on fire. I bite my lip so hard I taste blood. Just when I think the pain's never going to end, she coats my knees with the wet leaves, and the pain disappears immediately. "Aloe," she says. "Helps with the healing."

"Thank you," I say, releasing the grip on my bottom lip and hoping she doesn't douse that in alcohol too.

"What's your name?"

"Ines." As the lie rolls off my tongue, I remember when Nick first asked my name on the bus, and how he stopped calling me princess, without me even noticing. *But where is he now? Is he even alive?*

"I'm Isabel," she says. "You're lucky I heard you scream-ing. What were you doing out there anyway? Those feral dogs would've killed you."

I squeeze my hands into fists to keep them from shak-ing. "I'm on my way to Rosales," I say, "to meet my uncle."

"For the Day of the Dead?"

That thing again. I nod.

"Well, you sure got lost. That's several hours away," Isabel says. "But let's get you inside, and then we can talk some more."

Isabel's house is just a square block of concrete, divided into four equal sections by four fading black sheets. It looks like it's been staged for a commercial, the ones promising a dollar a day will save a child.

In the middle of the tiny front room is a wood fire. A tin bucket boils in the blue part of the flame, pale chicken legs flopping out the sides, and a covered ceramic bowl is nestled in the fire beside it. Around the fire, there's a small folding table, two plastic chairs, and a basket of chopped wood.

It takes all my energy not to look shocked. *People really live like this?*

At my house, the kitchen has its own wing, with a walk-in freezer and a temperature-controlled wine cellar. It's so far away from my room you have to scream for anyone to hear you. The memory of my pink bedroom and the life I left behind prickles through my bones and raises goose bumps on my skin. It feels like I've been gone for years, not days. *Will I ever find Isla Rosales, Roberto, the safe house? Will I ever get to go home?* I glance around the strange little room again, the sides closed in by faded black sheets, and a shiver courses through my body.

"You must be hungry." Isabel pulls a chair inches from the flames. "Sit here and eat." She scoops brown goop from a ceramic bowl on the fire. "Chicken in *mole negra.*"

With a grateful nod, I stuff a hunk of chicken covered in mud into my mouth. It tastes like a melted Snickers bar with a smoky, spicy ending.

Isabel makes a bed for Honey near the fire out of ratty blankets, and he lies down and shuts his eyes. "I'll get you some clean clothes," she says, pushing the sheet aside and grabbing something from the other room. "Try this," Isabel says, handing me a white cotton dress and then disappearing through the black sheet.

"Thanks." My teeth are chattering as I pull off my clothes and step into the dress, which fits perfectly. I sit down and let the heat from the fire surround me, seeping up my legs, warming chilled bones I didn't know I had. *And my God, does it feel good.* "Yessss." I sigh, letting the heat seep through the cracks in my toes, under my armpits, around my freezing cold ribs. *Ahhh, bliss.*

Besides the crackling of the fire, there's this dreamy silence, the kind of "on the moon" feeling you only get before you fall asleep. I imagine Nick's arms around me, nestling my head into his strong chest . . . *Don't think about him.* I breathe deeply, feeling air fill my lungs and clear my head. *Maybe Isabel will help me find Roberto, and he'll find Nick.* I see Mary's note in my mind, and I grasp on to it like it's my last bit of sanity: *Take any ferry to Isla Rosales. Roberto will meet you on the dock. He'll be wearing a cowboy hat.* I sink deeper into the warmth of the fire, my muscles slowly relaxing, letting the heat play over my face. *Roberto will know what to do.*

My head drops to my chest, and I let my eyelids close. I'm drifting in and out of a drowsy, peaceful sleep when I hear Isabel's voice float toward me, her syllables curving around unfamiliar words.

"What'd you say?" I ask.

The talking stops. There's a brief silence, then somebody answers back.

Somebody besides Isabel.

Is there someone else here? My eyes snap open, but I can't see past the black sheets closing me in on three sides. *Anybody could be back there. What was I thinking?* This strange house in the middle of nowhere, the kind woman who takes me in for no reason—how could I fall for this? I'm totally in the part of the horror film where the innocent girl walks into the killer's house while the audience yells, "Run away!" at the screen. "Isabel? Is there someone else here?" I ask, jumping to my feet.

"Just Abuelita," Isabel says, pushing the sheet aside, and yelling, "Abuelita!" loud enough to wake the dead. "My grandmother's partly deaf. Come with me."

When I step through the black sheet into the other room, the oldest woman I've ever seen is crouching behind an antique loom, the kind you'd see in a Brothers Grimm fairy tale. When she sees me, she pulls her hands out of a bucket filled with blue liquid. It smells like something is rotting, and I hope it's not her.

Trying not to hold my nose, I ask, "What is that?"

"Indigo dye. Abuelita's the best weaver in the region," Isabel says, pointing to the loom. "People come from all over Mexico for portraits of their families, of the saints." Her voice brims with pride. "We make especially good business during the Day of the Dead, when rich people want portraits for their altars."

"*Angelita*," the old woman murmurs, pulling her hands out of the bucket, her fingers dyed blue from mixing indigo. She doesn't bother to wipe them on her apron, just reaches up and traces the blue dye onto my face. "*Siéntate, angelita.*"

"What's an *angelita*?" I ask Isabel, staring at Abuelita's eyes. They're blue with lines of white cracks, like the edges of worn floor tile.

"Abuelita's old. She's talking nonsense." Isabel shrugs. She hands Abuelita a towel to wipe her hands, but Abuelita waves it away, her eyes focused on my face.

"Why do you say that?" I ask, taking the towel and wiping the indigo off my cheek.

"Because she called you an *angelita*. But an *angelita* is a dead child."

"Are you okay?" Isabel asks, leading me back through the curtain and settling my shivering body by the fire. She wraps a thick cotton shawl around me, but it doesn't help: I'm cold *inside*.

"Uh-huh," I reply. But I'm not okay. I'm terrified that Abuelita can see my future, can sense what's coming. "Is Abuelita a psychic?" I ask. Isabel looks at me strangely. In my world that's not a weird question. Mom visited dozens of psychics on Hollywood Boulevard to commune with the universe, although none of them predicted her death. Personally, I don't believe in psychic power, but Mom believed that everyone has some power, like people who know who's calling before they pick up the phone. She called that latent power. I don't have it. Things always surprise me, like a blow to the head.

"Psychic?" Isabel doesn't seem to know the word in English. She turns it over on her tongue, like a particularly unpleasant candy.

"Fortune-teller?" I make the image of a glass ball with my hands.

"No," she says sternly. "Only God knows the future."

Here's one thing I hate: awkward silences. I'll take fake compliments and knife-edged air-kisses over them any day. "So . . . um . . . I want to thank you," I stutter, "for saving me out there."

"It was nothing," Isabel says.

Nothing? I beg to differ. Where I come from, helping an old lady across the street is a stretch, but taking someone into your home? Unthinkable.

"Many people get lost out here, mostly tourists following the monarchs," Isabel says. "Since I'm the only one on this side of the mountain, I keep an eye out for people who need help."

People who need help. Like me. I never thought I'd be someone who "needed help." But Isabel's fed me, clothed me, bandaged my wounds. *What would I do if I found a bleeding girl outside my house? Call the police? Scream bloody murder? Certainly not invite her in and give her my new dress.*

I'm ashamed of myself, thinking that I'm putting her in danger. I try to swallow the lump that's building in my throat, but I can't. The priest was right; I'm a danger to everyone around me.

My mind strays back to Nick—his teasing grin, his

shaggy black hair, the way his arms fit around me like a life jacket, keeping me afloat. But then I picture the empty space on the dirt road, and pain rips across my chest.

"I should go," I say, getting up from my chair.

Isabel looks at me in confusion. "But there's nowhere to go. The nearest village is ten kilometers away. Besides, most of the villagers already left for the cemetery, or are leaving in a few hours, like me."

That stops me. "Why the cemetery?"

"Because tomorrow the dead come home."

The dead come home? Despite the heat from the fire, a shiver trembles through my body, and I drop back into my chair. *But the dead can't come home—only the undead.* There are very few things that scare me as much as the undead. After starring in *Zombie Killer* as a young girl who kills half of America's undead, I couldn't sleep for weeks. On set, zombies crawled out of tombs and dug up graves, bleeding from the mouth. At home, they lived under my bed, fangs dripping with human flesh, waiting for my tiny ankle to slip to the floor.

"You mean the undead? Like zombies?" I ask, studying Isabel's face to make sure she's joking.

"*¿Zombi?* No. *Almas.* The spirits of people who've died." She stirs the chicken in the tin bucket; its legs spin round and round. "That's why Abuelita called you an *angelita.* She's old, and she gets confused sometimes. And since you're wearing Paloma's dress," Isabel says sadly, "she thinks that you're Paloma, back for the Day of the Dead."

"Who?"

"My niece. Six months ago, she disappeared."

Chapter Fifteen

SIX MONTHS AGO? SHOCK SHOOTS through me, catching all my nerves on fire. Her niece disappeared out here, in the middle of nowhere? At the same time my mom was killed?

"Would you like to see Paloma?" she asks. I nod, and then I follow Isabel through the black sheet into a room glowing with candlelight. A towering altar of wooden crates is covered with pictures of Mexican movie stars torn out of magazines, cracked plastic cases of eye shadow, and a giant weaving of a smiling teenage girl.

"Meet Paloma," she says, pointing to the weaving.

Paloma's so—beautiful. Her skin is a glistening bronze,

and she has these irresistible pouty lips and short, shiny black hair. *She should have been in movies.*

"A couple of years ago, when my sister left Paloma with me, I thought she would return for her," Isabel says. "My sister's work usually kept her away for a few months at a time, but that time . . . she just never came home."

"She wasn't a weaver?"

Isabel shakes her head. "Aurora worked for Marcos, a very important man in this community. He owns the businesses, the land, the cemetery and funeral homes, everything. He even puts on charity events in the church, but all for a price."

"Which is?"

"Silence. About who and what he steals," Isabel says. "Marcos makes it easy. You're either silent or silenced."

"Silenced." I shiver as I stare at the altar, trying to put the pieces together in my mind.

"Abuelita built an altar because she doesn't think Paloma's still alive, but I do," Isabel says. "So when I was lighting the candles on the altar tonight, and I heard the dogs . . . somehow I thought . . . and then I found you."

Right then I know I'm a disappointment. That every moment she spends with me reminds her of who I could have been. Sadness fills me, sadness for both of us.

"I'm sorry," I say. "I'm sorry I'm not who you were looking for."

Isabel stares at me for a moment, and then pulls me into her arms. I hold tightly to her, uncertain what I'm supposed to do.

When she finally pulls away, she looks me in the eye. "Don't ever say that again. God gives us miracles, even if they're not the ones we expect."

Before I can tell her that I'm the furthest thing from a miracle, Isabel ducks into the other room and returns with an old-fashioned radio. It's the kind you see in movies, those World War II ones where a spy has to break an enemy's code.

"I check it every evening to see if they've found out anything about Paloma." Isabel sets it down and turns the knob, and the radio crackles to life. At first it's only static, and the occasional mariachi band slipping in and out of tune. My mind starts to wander, imagining what it must be like to live out here, with the radio as your only entertainment. No DVDs of dead moms. No internet rumors. No news shows about stars being murdered. But then I hear my name, and I realize I'm a fool: when a star dies, everyone can see it.

I hear my name only once before the radio slips into static again. The static is tangible; it's like being lost in a sandstorm, following the sound of one tinny voice. Isabel shakes the radio and the voice comes back to life.

"Actriz Vivian Divine fue encontrado muerta en Norte Hollywood."

"What's she saying?" I ask, trying not to sound too desperate.

She listens for a second, a frown creasing her face. "They're saying that a young movie star was just found dead. Stabbed in the back."

The whole world thinks I'm dead. Maybe that's what Abuelita meant by a dead child—maybe I'm dead inside.

"*Pobre niña,*" Isabel sighs. "She was only sixteen."

Then Dad's voice, like the deep undercurrent of a wave, comes on the radio for a second before the announcer translates what he is saying into Spanish.

"*Ofrezco cincuenta millones de dólares a quien que encuentra su asesino,*" the tinny voice says.

"What did that man say?" I ask, forcing myself to slow down and stifle the desperate need to know that's tearing through me.

"The girl's father is offering fifty million dollars to whoever finds her killer," Isabel says.

Dad is safe. Thinking of him, something tears at my heart, like those butterflies, all billion of them, jumping into the sky.

Isabel turns the knob, and silence crackles like electricity around us. "Enough bad news," she says. "You're too young to hear such things."

I wish I were. I wish I could go back to the time before Mom died, when I never thought about murder and death, when I was still young enough to trust the world.

"We'd better get ready to go," Isabel continues, standing and picking up the radio. "It'll take a couple of hours to get to Rosales. If you need to use the outhouse before we leave, it's right outside."

Even though the last thing I want to do is walk alone to the outhouse after my near miss with the feral dogs, I decide to brave it. *If I made it across Mexico, I can handle an outhouse at night.* I smile at Isabel and walk outside, steeling myself for the smell. It's unpleasant, and stinky, and drafty in all the wrong places, but it's not as bad as I thought it would be, and I'm even a little proud of myself.

On the way back to the house, my flashlight scatters shadows across the mountain. As I walk gingerly through the trees, I see a faded beam of light in the woods. *Is someone else lost in the woods?*

The light is pretty far away, but it's coming fast, getting brighter by the second. Then the beam doubles, and there are two streams of light.

Those aren't flashlights: they're headlights.

And they're coming straight for me.

A cold pit opens up in my stomach when I see Isabel holding the front door open. "I'm not sure who it is," Isabel says, ushering me inside. "People don't usually come out this far, and if they do, they don't bring good news."

She shuts the door behind her, crosses the kitchen in two steps, and pulls the sheet to the altar room. "Just stay here until I tell you to come out." As Isabel pulls the sheet closed between us, tires squeal to a stop. I crawl over to the altar and blow the candles out, Paloma's beautiful face blinking into darkness.

A car door slams and footsteps grind across the gravel. I cower back in the darkness, watching the front door through a small tear in the sheet.

There's a knock on the door, but before Isabel can move to open it, a uniformed guard pulls the door open and a man enters.

The man who walks in might look ordinary at first glance, but you'd look again. His pale gray eyes shimmer in the firelight like melted silver. His red silk suit matches his ruby-topped cane, and a long, unlit cigarette dangles from his lips above a thin gray mustache. When he moves, one leg drags behind him just slightly enough that I wonder if I imagined it.

"Señor Marcos," Isabel says in surprise, quickly brushing off the kitchen chair for him to sit down.

"Isabel," Marcos says, ignoring the chair, and stepping up to kiss her on one cheek.

"¿Cómo puedo ayudarse?" Isabel whimpers.

Marcos paces around the room, glancing in each dark corner. *What is he looking for?* He nods at his guard, who quickly moves forward, striking his lighter with nervous hands. Marcos doesn't break eye contact with Isabel as he sucks the end of the cigarette until the red tip glows. "*¿Está listo?*" he asks, smoke leaking out of the corners of his mouth.

On the other side of the curtain, I hear the loom start to pound.

"*Lo siento, señor,*" Isabel says. "*Mañana.*"

Marcos nods at her, and then gestures to the guard. The guard leaves, quickly returning with a paper sack of apples and a plastic grocery bag crammed full of marigold petals.

"*Para Los Muertos,*" Marcos says. "*Para todos en Rosales.*"

"*Gracias, señor,*" Isabel says, bowing her head.

"*Y esto es para su trabajo,*" Marcos pulls a roll of money out of his suit pocket, and something falls unnoticed to the floor. He peels off a few bills, and puts the money roll back in his pocket. "*Adiós,*" he says, taking a last drag of his cigarette and holding it out to the guard between two fingers. The guard quickly takes it from him.

When Marcos turns around to leave, the guard flicks the lit cigarette toward the open doorway, but it falls short, landing in Honey's bed of blankets. The lamb squeals in fear, and the smell of burning fabric fills the air. Isabel hurries over to stamp it out, but Marcos halts abruptly and holds his hand up in a stop signal. He slowly turns around and picks up the cigarette.

"*Idiota*," he says to his guard. Marcos calmly takes his guard's hand and presses the lit cigarette into it until the guard cries out in pain.

"*No, señor*," Isabel pleads.

"*¿Sí?*" Marcos asks, and Isabel nods. Marcos lifts the burning cigarette off the man's palm. "*Lo siento*, Isabel," Marcos says, glaring at the guard.

"*Lo siento*," the guard repeats sheepishly.

Marcos waits until the guard grounds out the fire under his boot and opens the door. Popping the cigarette back into his mouth, Marcos goes out into the dark night, the guard slinking out behind him.

After I hear his car squeal away, I crawl through the sheet into the main room. Isabel is still standing in the same place, staring at the door as if he's going to yank it open and stab her in the heart.

My eyes are locked on the thing that fell from his pocket. It's near the fire, half-hidden beneath a leg of the rickety card table. As I get closer, my cheek suddenly burns like he just slapped me. Because lying there, looking completely out of place in this tiny hut in the middle of nowhere, is a rose, carved out of a single pink diamond.

Chapter Sixteen

VISIONS OF THE LAST DAY I saw Mom swim through my mind. I see her standing in the doorway in her white shawl, her pink diamond earrings dangling from her ears. *If Mom was wearing those earrings the day she was kidnapped, why did Marcos have one of them?*

"Are you okay?" Isabel asks.

I shake my head. *I have to find out why Marcos had my mom's earring. He may know something about what happened to Mom, but I don't know who he is or how to find him, and I can't speak his language.* I watch Isabel's legs tremble beneath her as she wraps Honey in a wool blanket. *I need Isabel's help, but I have to admit who I am in order to do that. Should I tell her? Didn't Mary say to tell no one, no matter who it was?* I glance at Isabel's shotgun, propped up beside the door, and quickly pick up Mom's earring. *But Isabel's taken care of me, and I have no other option.*

"Isabel," I say, trying to make my voice calm, despite the panic coursing through my body. "I'm not who I said I am. My name is not Ines."

Isabel stops and stares at me. "Are you a runaway? Are your parents looking for you?"

I have to draw in breath to get out the next few words. "My real name is Vivian Divine."

"The girl on the radio?" Isabel says, staring at me like I just fell out of the sky. "The movie star?"

I nod.

"But you're . . . dead." Isabel backs away from me then, as if Abuelita was right and she's looking at a ghost. *A ghost who was murdered violently in a country far away from here. An angry ghost looking for revenge.*

"I'm not dead! Someone faked my death."

"Why would they do that?"

"I don't know. I don't know why anyone would want me dead." My voice is rising to a hysterical pitch. "But they killed my mom too."

"*¿Tu madre?*" Her voice is doubtful. "Why?"

"I don't know why. But the police were involved, and the FBI too."

Isabel takes a few steps toward me. "The FBI?"

I tell Isabel about my last few days: receiving the death threat, fleeing L.A. in disguise, hitchhiking down here, flipping Scars's car and escaping into the woods. I don't mention Nick. If I say his name, I might break down. "So I have nowhere to turn," I finish, "but to you."

"Why me?"

I hold out my hand, showing her the pink diamond earring. "This was my mom's earring," I tell her, trying not to choke up. "One of the earrings she was wearing when she disappeared. Marcos dropped it just now."

Isabel is quiet for a minute, staring at the earring in my palm. A silence settles over us, as uncomfortable as a wet feather bed. "You've lied to me about everything," Isabel says. "Why should I trust you now?"

"Um . . ." I can't think of anything I've done to make her believe me.

Isabel glances down at my muddy shoes with the gold Gs on them, and then she shakes her head like she's going against her better judgment. "Okay. Let's say, for a moment, that I believe you. Why would Marcos have your mother's earring?"

"I don't know. But is it possible he knows something about my mom's death?"

"It's possible," Isabel says. "But it's more likely that his men hijacked a truckload of jewelry, and this was in it."

I imagine a truck bed of jewels, packed in darkness, crossing the border. "True. He may just be a thief. But if you can help me—"

"No!" Isabel says. "He's too powerful."

"I'm not asking you to confront him," I say. *Just to risk your life for a girl you barely know, a girl who leaves a trail of bodies behind her.* "I just want you to take me to him," I continue, completely aware that Isabel may end up dead in a field, covered in butterflies. *Am I a bad person for wanting her to help me?*

"You saw what I turn into when he's around," she says. "I didn't even want to do this weaving for him, but—"

"What weaving?"

Isabel leads me through the curtain into Abuelita's weaving room, where a rug, at least two feet long, is stretched taut across the wooden loom. Even though the wide wooden plank covers the middle section, I can still see the golden halo and the pale blue veil draped around Mother Mary's face. "A month ago, Marcos commissioned this weaving from us," Isabel says. "It's not quite ready, but I told him I'd bring it to him tomorrow morning."

I turn away from the weaving to stare into Isabel's frightened eyes. "He might not know anything, but he had the earring my mom was wearing when she was kidnapped!" I insist. "Even if he bought it, he bought it from someone. And if he got it himself . . ." I shiver. "You've got to find out for me."

Isabel shakes her head, her hands a blockade in front of her. "No. It's too risky."

I glance behind me at the black sheet, remembering

how the candle flame danced on the altar, highlighting Paloma's beautiful face. "If you could find out what happened to Paloma," I ask, locking eyes with Isabel, "would you?"

"I guess I would," she whispers.

"Then help me!"

"I already said no, Ines, or Vivian, or whatever your name is." She turns and picks up a stack of white spindly candles from the floor and pushes through the black sheet into the kitchen. "I have to get ready," she says. "And if you're coming to Rosales, you'd better get ready, too."

I wrap Mom's earring in a small piece of dyed yarn lying on the floor, stick it in my bra, and follow her into the kitchen. In silence, we pile bags of marigold petals, white candles, and bruised red apples onto the table, until its almost overflowing. I'm starting to wonder if she's angry enough to leave me behind when she clears her throat.

"So I was thinking," Isabel says, "about Paloma. I haven't wanted to admit it," she adds, tears in her voice, "but Paloma is probably dead." She focuses on stacking the candles perfectly into a cloth bag. "But if you could help me find out what happened to Paloma, and you didn't, that wouldn't make you a very good person."

Maybe I'm not a very good person. Maybe I would run away scared, like you're doing.

"And if you were afraid," Isabel continues, "and you

couldn't get past it, I'd call you a coward." She looks up then, but she's far away, in a place I can't see. "I'm not a coward."

A few minutes later, I follow Isabel out of the house into the dark night, a pile of candles in my arms. Crickets are chirping and the sound of howling lingers in the night sky.

"Should I put these in the car?" I ask, praying that, by the time we get to Rosales, Roberto will still be waiting at the dock.

Isabel puts her fingers in her mouth and blows one long, piercing whistle, and an old brown workhorse pads up. "Meet Tenorio," she says, patting his fuzzy brown nose.

"Oh, no, I don't ride horses," I insist. The terror of my horse scene in *Abandoned*, my Oscar-nominated role as a teenager in a postapocalyptic world, comes back to me: a disobedient horse, sailing through the air before landing on my back. Weeks of physical therapy later, I swore I'd never ride a horse again. It took my agent months to secure that "No Horse" clause on all my contracts.

"That's the only way to get there," Isabel says.

"Then I'll walk," I say, realizing I've sunk to an all-time low if I'm offering to continue *walking* up a mountain. At home, I'd rather die than make the three-block trek to the nearest nail salon.

As Isabel ties the bags onto Tenorio's back, Abuelita toddles up, the weaving for Marcos cradled in her arms like a baby. "*Completo*," Abuelita says.

Isabel takes the weaving from her and ties it on top of the bundle. "*Te amo*," she says, kissing Abuelita on the forehead. Abuelita squeezes my hand before she wanders back into the house. "She's too old to come," Isabel says, "but she'll take care of your lamb until you can come back for him. Do you want to say good-bye?"

Guilt leaks into me from all sides. *Until I come back for him. Both of us know that's never going to happen.* I shake my head. "I hate good-byes," I say. "They kill me every time."

Isabel climbs onto Tenorio and kicks his side. He plods slowly away from the house, and I drop into step behind him, making sure his big brown butt is more than kicking distance away from my face. But as I follow his U-shaped hoof prints up the mountain, I realize that what I said about good-byes isn't true. Good-byes have cracked me open wide and rained salt on my wounds, but maybe I'm stronger than I thought I was, because they haven't killed me—yet.

Chapter Seventeen

I'VE BEEN FOLLOWING THE BUTT of the horse for over two hours, cursing myself for ever leaving L.A. in the first place, when we finally reach the top of the mountain. *If our bus hadn't broken down, I'd be safe with Roberto by now. But then I never would have met Nick, who can make me tingle just by looking at me. If he's even still alive.*

Below us, rows of whitewashed buildings, dug out of the rock face, shine under a sky thickening with stars. Dark mist clings to the surrounding mountain cliffs. On the far side of the village is a black drop-off, a giant crater in the mountainside. It's dotted with tiny lights, like stars fallen to earth.

"Welcome to Rosales," Isabel says. She takes Tenorio's reins and leads him down the hill, and I follow, feeling pleasantly removed from the world up here. I try to memorize the small streets, the heavy mist, the smell of fried food, Isabel's long black braids waving in the breeze. It's almost peaceful.

Peace never lasts as long as I'd like. Before I know it, my massage is over, my spa day has ended, and my feeling of relaxation slips away. But this is like smashing peace until it shatters through me like splinters. Because as I step off the hillside, into the street, the world explodes with sound.

A band pushes past me, trombones wailing in my ears, drums pounding so hard they make my heart beat faster. Skeletons swirl around me, their sinister faces pressing in on me; red devils writhe across the pavement; black-shrouded skulls grin at me maniacally.

Isabel reaches into one of the saddlebags on Tenorio's back. "Try this on," she says, handing me a mask draped with several inches of white lace. "It was Paloma's."

An unsettled feeling creeps over me, and I suddenly realize Abuelita was right when she called me an *angelita*. In Paloma's dress and mask, I must look like her from head to ankle; my sneakers are the only thing left of the real me. It's like I've finally disappeared—completely.

"I'm glad you're here," Isabel says, and I wonder if she's glad because I'm a stand-in for her missing niece.

"Me too," I say, realizing I don't care, because in a way, Isabel's a stand-in too, for the mom that died and took part of me with her.

Once the parade passes, Isabel leads Tenorio out into the middle of the narrow street. I follow her, thinking about what a crew we must make: a horse dying on its feet, a middle-aged weaver, and me—a hunted movie star, probably being watched right now.

I glance around at the groups of people lingering in front of houses, expecting to see the barrels of guns poking out through corner windows. Instead, pasted up in each window is a red-and-black poster of a man and woman in a passionate embrace, with the words "*Don Juan Tenorio*" written underneath.

"People come from all over the country to see it," Isabel says. "*Don Juan* used to be performed every Day of the Dead in towns across the country. Most of them have lost the tradition, but Marcos has kept this one alive," she adds. "Have you heard of it?"

I nod. "Vaguely." *If vaguely means every line in the script, backward and forward.* I suddenly miss the back lot, the lights and the hassle and the scripts. I even miss Pierre and his cocky attitude, and Mary constantly in my shadow, and Dad's stupid angel T-shirts. *Maybe they're kinda cool, after all.*

We turn a corner into a cobblestone plaza. It's packed

with food stands selling tamales, hot chocolate, and vats of fried grasshoppers. Their little bodies jump as they're fried. Kids in costumes run ahead of us, their laughter ringing off the buildings. The smell of chocolate is thick in the air.

"The children's parade's about to start," Isabel says, tying Tenorio to a fence on the edge of the square, lined with a dozen other horses.

I watch the kids bunched together at a roped-off entrance to the square. It looks like Halloween in L.A.: kids dressed as ghosts, superheroes, even a little bride.

"Cute bride," I say, pointing to the girl in a white dress and veil.

"She's not a bride," Isabel says. "She's Dona Blanca, the Girl in White. The myth says that Dona Blanca dances with the best-looking boy in town, but when he brags about it, everyone says he was dancing alone. He realizes she's a ghost, and that death has come for him."

I look closer at the little girl in the Dona Blanca costume. She's pulling at her veil, trying to straighten it, when the lace lifts off her face.

It's the girl from the truck.

Chapter Eighteen

I'M SHOCKED BY HOW HAPPY I am to see her. *She's safe. I'll never find her dead in a field because of me.* Tension falls off my body in waves. *And maybe she's even seen Nick!* "I have to talk to that girl," I say, and dash across the square before Isabel can follow.

Ducking under the rope into the crowd of children, I feel like I've just landed in Peter Pan's Neverland. Children swarm around my knees, giggling and singing. Plump mothers bicker over their kids—adjusting collars, spitting on their hands to rub chocolate off little faces.

"Hey, you! Little girl!" I yell, pushing through the miniature crowd until I'm standing next to her. "I have Honey," I say.

The girl looks up, and I'd recognize that smile with the missing front teeth anywhere. Then I lean down and take off my mask. Her smile dies instantly, and her lower lip starts to quiver. She dashes away from me, pushing through the waist-high crowd.

"Wait!" I run after her, a giant in a sea of midgets. When I catch up to her at the back of the parade, she hunches over like a cornered animal, tears gathering on her cheeks. *Why is she so scared?*

"Honey is alive," I say, but she just stares at me, confused. "Baaa," I say, and give her a thumbs-up.

She breaks into a huge smile. "Okay?"

"Okay," I assure her. *Now for the serious sign language.* I point at the girl and say, "Have you?" Then I touch the corner of my eye and say, "Seen?" I pause. She looks at me curiously. I'm not sure what to do next, so I put my hand to my heart and say, "Nick?"

She shakes her head.

"Oh," I sigh, disappointed. *What did I expect? She'd point across the square and there he'd be, waiting for me with open arms, when he's probably dead in a bush on the side of the road?*

She points to me now, and then to her masked face. *I guess it's her turn to play this game.* The little girl pulls her mask off. She has a long red cut down the side of her face.

I get chill bumps up the back of my neck. *Did Scars do this to her?* My cheek burns as I imagine a knife ripping through her skin, scarring her forever. *Was it because of me?*

"Who did that to you?" I ask.

She tilts her head as if she's waiting for the Spanish version to fall out of the sky and into her ear. I crouch down in front of her and point to my face. Then I draw a moon-shaped line from my forehead to my chin, just like hers.

"No," she says, shaking her head and looking into the crowd nervously, where her mom is pushing frantically through the other mothers.

"You can't tell me?"

The little girl glances at her mom, and then she gets that devilish gleam kids get when they know they're doing something wrong. Her hair tickles my cheek as she leans in closely and whispers in my ear: "*La Família de Muerta.*"

La what?

Before I can think of more sign language, her mom's hand closes around her tiny arm. The mom glares at me, her eyes narrowing into thin slits of red-hot anger.

"*¡Déjanos en paz!*" she shrieks. I flinch as her breath washes over me, a mix of coffee and bitter chilies. As the other mothers turn to glare at me, I slink away, wishing I could just disappear.

Then someone blows a horn to start the parade, and the mothers quickly lose interest. Only one person is left staring at me, her mouth hanging open in surprise: Isabel.

Isabel wades through the kids in costumes, the weaving

tucked tightly under her arm. "How do you know that girl?" Isabel asks, squinting at me like she's trying to figure out a complicated crossword puzzle.

The children's parade is partway across the square by now. The mothers are running ahead, trying to keep the kids in line as they march in a large circle around the square.

"When the bus broke down, we hitched a ride in her family's truck."

"We?"

"My friend. He helped me after my bag was stolen."

"Where is he now?" Isabel asks.

I shake my head. "I don't know. He was just . . . gone. I wish . . ." *I wish he were alive now, charming people with his sly smile and his huge, well-hidden heart.* "I wish that girl knew where he was. But she just muttered something in Spanish."

"What did she say?"

"*La Família de Muerta.*"

Isabel chokes on my words. "What did you say?"

Before I can answer, ten-foot-tall skeletons hobble toward me, carrying a giant coffin. "*La Família de Muerta,*" I say, ducking under the coffin so it doesn't whack me in the head. I glance straight up into the gaping eye sockets of a skeleton, peering down at me through the glass bottom of the coffin.

"We can't talk here," Isabel says. She pushes her way

through the crowd, and I try to follow, but a cart dangling with ceramic skeletons stops abruptly in front of me. The skeletons' limbs run into each other, their bones clattering like funeral bells. An old woman thrusts a skeleton in my face, its bobbing head nearly amputated off its fragile neck.

"¿Cómprelo?" she asks.

I shake my head and push past her, spotting Isabel turning off the main square. I cut into the alley, and quite suddenly, we're alone.

Away from the crowds, the darkness is unsettling. The smell of the lake is stronger here, a mix of fish and kerosene.

I rub Paloma's white lace mask nervously between my fingers. I know I should put it on, but it's itchy, and I can't see out of it anyway. "What are we doing here?" I ask. "Waiting for muggers?"

"La Familia de Muerta is the most powerful mafia in Mexico," Isabel whispers. "Maybe the world. They're based in this region, but they've never been arrested, because they own the police." Isabel looks around nervously, and then leans in closely to whisper in my ear. "Nobody messes with them, or they're found with their throat slit on the side of the road."

I shudder at the memory of butterfly wings on the FBI agent's dead eyes. I can still smell his sweet, rotting stench, and I almost gag. "Why do they kill people?"

"Because they feel betrayed or lied to, or because someone discovered one of their smuggling routes. They smuggle everything illegal: drugs, weapons, people."

"People?"

"Kidnapping. They even kidnapped the daughter of our last president," Isabel says, her eyes wide. "They can get to anybody."

A few minutes later, my heart is pounding a thousand miles an hour as we wind through the tiny streets toward the lake. *Anybody. They can get to anybody.* With every step closer to the dock, the aroma gets stronger, until the heavy kerosene scent slowly mixes with the smell of bleach and dead fish. Isabel refuses to say anything else, murmuring how "anybody could be listening."

When we finally reach the harbor, I'm relieved to be surrounded by people, sound, even piles of dead fish, although the odor is suffocating. Despite the smell, the harbor is lovely: just a small wooden boardwalk crowded with villagers, all dressed in bleached white clothing. I feel like I'm in a laundry detergent commercial.

"Why are they all wearing white?" I ask Isabel, glad to have something safe to talk about.

"Most of the natives are indigenous. That's all they wear."

Only one outfit? How surprisingly hassle free. *Just white. I think I'll wear white today.*

On the dark lake, fishing boats, their beige butterfly nets covering the water like giant hearts, mingle with tiny wooden canoes and larger passenger boats. I can't help but marvel at the beauty of it all: the white of the clothing, the black of the water, the swaying of the wooden oars in the lake, the kerosene lamps burning on the sides of the boats.

"That's Isla Rosales," Isabel says, pointing to an island in the middle of the lake. White houses climb up from the shore in uneven rows around a white marble staircase, disappearing into the star-strewn sky. "The cemetery's at the top," she says, pointing to where the moon is hanging in a glowing ball above the island. "That's where we're headed."

"Do we have to go to the cemetery? Can't we just deliver the weaving to Marcos, and find out if he knows anything?"

"He won't be here until tomorrow, like the rest of the men," Isabel says, shifting the bags to her other shoulder and tucking the weaving under her arm like buried treasure. "Tonight we spend the night in the cemetery with our loved ones."

I'd refuse to go to the island at all, but the thought of finding Roberto is enough to keep my legs moving. *The quicker I find him, the better. Because as soon as I find Roberto, he'll confront Marcos about Mom's earring, help me find Nick, and this whole stupid mess will be over. And not a moment too soon.*

Seagulls sweep down over our heads as a fishing boat pulls up to the dock, loaded with live squirming fish.

"*Boletos! Boletos!*" fishermen call, pulling their boats up to the dock and gesturing for us to choose between them. In the dark night, the kerosene lamps on the boats' hulls glimmer like fireflies.

"I'll buy tickets," Isabel says, ignoring the fishermen and walking toward a little wooden shack with the sign: "*Boletos.*"

My mind is whirling as I look around me: in the light of a rusty streetlamp, there's an old man selling candy skeletons, towers of bird cages balancing on a bicycle, little girls licking chocolate off their fingers, their braids almost reaching the ground. I glance back at Isabel, who's now at the *boletos* shack, haggling with a boatman for tickets.

"Ines." The word is whispered so softly I think it's the wind. But then I hear it again: "Ines."

I look out at the boats bobbing in the water. There are men chanting the price of a trip across the lake, people climbing into boats, their white clothes dipping in the water, an old man smoking a pipe, and him.

Nick.

Chapter Nineteen

I CAN'T BELIEVE MY EYES. I've never been so happy to see someone in my life. I blink and pinch myself, in case he's an illusion, but he doesn't go away. He floats a little closer, his tiny wooden boat barely big enough for him.

I want to run, to dive into his arms, but I'm afraid to attract attention. So I walk slowly, casually, and climb into the boat beside him. The wooden bench is damp under my thighs, but I hardly notice. We're only inches away, his skin radiating heat near my skin.

"You're alive." Adrenaline races through my body, quivering every inch of me. I want to trace my finger up his arm, over his shoulders, up his neck, onto his lips . . .

"I am now," Nick says, and smiles a heartbreaking grin. I glance down at the lake, watching how the kerosene lamp throws his reflection in the water, my blush too bright to look him in the eyes.

"Where'd you get this boat?"

"Borrowed it."

I don't care if he stole it. He's here. With me.

"How'd you get here?"

"Long story," Nick says.

"Me too," I sigh, finally drawing my eyes up to his. "I'm just glad you're not hurt." I don't want to tear my eyes from his ever again. *He could've been killed because of me.* But he wasn't, and now he's here, and I'm never letting him go. And by the way he's looking at me, I don't think he wants to let me go either.

"I've been so scared," Nick says. "I was afraid that you—"

"Ines?" Isabel calls. She's on the dock, two tickets in her hand. Her bags sag around her feet, apples leaking out the sides. She looks so helpless, standing there alone, her eyes roaming over the dozens of crowded boats.

"I'll be right back," I say to Nick as I climb out of the boat, leaving my mask on the bench beside him. "Isabel!" I call over the crowd. She turns and looks at me as I jog up to her, her face tight with worry.

"Where have you been?"

"Remember the friend I told you about? The one who

helped me when my bag was stolen?"

"*Sí.*" Isabel nods, her voice heavy with confusion.

"He's here! I just want to ride over to the island with him," I say. "I'll meet you on the dock, I promise."

"Too crowded. We'll never find each other there," Isabel says. "Are you sure this is a good idea?"

I nod. *Her concern would be sweet any other time, but now I just want to get back to Nick.*

"Okay," she says. "Just meet me at the entrance to the cemetery. I'll be easy to find." She gestures to her bright purple dress.

"I'll be there," I say. *With Roberto, after I find him on the dock.*

"I understand," she says, glancing at Nick's boat. He's looking out at the lake, his back to us. She squeezes my hand. "It's always about a boy, isn't it?"

As Isabel turns and hands her ticket to a boat conductor, I nod, trying to contain my smile. *I can ride with Nick. She's so cool! Mary would have totally broken his arm and dragged him screaming from the boat by now.*

After Isabel waves, I sprint back to Nick's boat and jump in. The boat rocks under us, the oars knocking lightly against the side, but I'm not scared. I have Nick back, and we'll find Roberto together. Maybe Nick can even help me find out what Marcos knows about Mom's death—if he knows anything at all.

* * *

As Nick rows us into the lake, weaving in and out of boats, I watch Isabel's boat float away, and soon we look like everyone else in the dark night: a small wooden boat among hundreds of small wooden boats.

I watch the stern slice through the dark water, the oars bringing up blackness and dumping it, again and again. There's so much I want to ask Nick, but I don't know where to start.

"What are you thinking about?" he asks, staring at the disappearing and reappearing wooden oars.

"Nick? After we found the, you know, body," I say, "what happened to you?"

He pulls his gaze from the water. I notice, for the first time, that he looks beat-up and exhausted. "I don't remember much. I know someone knocked me out."

How terrifying. My hand automatically reaches for his arm. I let my fingers rest on his damp skin, feeling the electricity move between us.

"I'm not sure how long I was out, but the next thing I knew, I was on the side of the road. And I got this."

Nick pulls the hair off his forehead. At his hairline is a deep purple bruise, crusted around the edges with dried blood. *It's my fault. He could've been killed because of me.* I touch his bruise lightly, but he still winces.

"Does it hurt?"

He shakes his head. "Not much."

I level him with my gaze, my eyebrows lifting in disbelief. He tries to look away, but there's something between us, an invisible magnet, and he's drawn back to me again.

"Maybe a little," he admits.

I smile at him on the outside, but inside I'm cursing at myself for getting him involved in something so dangerous. *Why did I have to meet Nick now, of all times? When just being around me could have gotten him killed?*

"So how'd you get here?" I ask, trying to keep the conversation away from me.

"I hitchhiked," he says, "hoping you'd made it here. I've been so worried about you."

"Me too. About you, I mean." I blush in the timid darkness. I want to tell him that I missed him every moment I was away from him, but I don't.

"What happened to you?" Nick asks, his voice so concerned it makes me want to cry.

Should I tell him that I'm not the girl I say I am; that there's someone who wants me dead, and almost killed him instead? Will he blame me? I glance at the wound on his forehead. *It's not worth taking the chance.* "I don't want to talk about it," I say. "Not now."

Nick nods and rows the boat farther into the lake. When we're far enough away from shore, and the land looks like a thousand twinkling fireflies, he rows us into a small rock cove. Nestled into a pocket of trees dripping with moss, I feel completely hidden from the world. Nick rests the oars on the edge of the boat, lowers the anchor, and blows out the kerosene lamp.

"I have to admit something," Nick says, and I wonder if it is anything compared to what I'd have to admit, if I had the courage to do so. "When I met you on the bus, I thought you were just another rich American," he continues. "But you're not. You're . . . different." Nick reaches for my hand, and I'm surprised by how soft his hand is, and how the warmth of his skin seeps into mine. "I think that ex-boyfriend of yours was a real fool, to let someone like you go," he says.

"Someone like me?"

"You may be all gristle, but you're pretty and kind and, um . . . a good listener, too."

Wow! Nicks thinks I'm pretty and kind and . . . what was the other one?

"I promised I'd get you here to meet your uncle, but I failed," Nick continues. "You could have died—"

I put my finger on his lips. "Shhhh . . ." I can feel the water rocking the boat beneath us. It feels unreal for a moment: Marcos, Scars, everything.

Everything but Nick.

"When nobody's watching," I say, "you're actually pretty sweet."

"Nobody can see us here," he whispers.

I've never been so glad to be invisible. I feel the strong muscles in his arms, the soft skin under his wrists. He sighs and runs his hand through my hair and down my arm, and then his fingers slide between mine.

The silence between us is as comfortable as my own skin. We wrap ourselves in it. His touch is so soft it feels like wind coming off the water. His scent—sweat, earth, and sunshine—tangles up with the smell of wet wood, and I close my eyes and breathe it in. I lean back against him, his hard chest holding us both up in the blackness of the boat.

I'm not sure how long we float there, in the safe, quiet darkness. I just know there's no place else I want to be. And I even start to believe a lie: that nobody can hurt me when he's around.

Drifting in the darkness, all I can see are the stars above me, below me, and inside of me. Make that exploding stars. Because he does just what he did in my dream: he turns me around and traces my lips with his fingertips. Then he leans into me, and I become his kiss.

When he becomes such a part of me that I can't remember my lips without his, he strips down to his boxers and slides into the black water.

"Ines," Nick whispers, only his eyes visible in the darkness.

My dress comes off easier than I had imagined,

making me grateful for the dark night between us. I wait until his back is turned, and then I wrap the yarn bundle with Mom's earring in my dress and slip into the cold water, welcoming it around my fevered skin. Alone with Nick in the chilly darkness, the rest of the world seems so far away.

I breathe in deeply, filling my lungs with air. My body is tiny, weightless. I feel like I'm floating through outer space, circling the planets, unattached to anything. Water flows through the spaces between my limbs; when they touch, they feel like silk.

He is floating near me; I can feel the heat of his body. He ripples through the water around me until we are touching, palm to palm, then cheek to cheek. We are the only people in the world.

I want to stay here forever, but my legs are already starting to get tired from treading water. He puts his arms around my waist, his fingers pressing against the band of my silk panties.

"*Tranquilo*," he says. I let my whole body relax. As I float on top of the water, my skin an impossible white in the moonlight, I let myself melt into his arms, and, for the first time since Mom died, I feel some of the ice crack inside me. Warmth flows through my chest, softening parts of me I thought I'd never feel again. That tiny flame, the one I felt in the field of butterflies, flickers more brightly, and I remember, for a brief second, what it felt like to be happy.

I lean back in his arms, and my chest feels lighter, as if part of the sadness that has been locked up in my body is pooling in the edges of my fingertips and toes, and drifting away, into the water.

I inhale slowly, and as my chest inflates, I let myself float on top of the water, and then I exhale, and let myself sink again, Nick's arms holding me the whole time.

Then the thought comes. But I don't think it. It flows through me, mixing with the water, until I can't tell if I'm inside or outside my body. *This is what love feels like.*

I want to lie in Nick's arms forever, but lake water is splashing into my mouth, so I exhale fully and let my legs sink into the water until we're chest to chest. Nick wraps one arm around me and pulls my body tightly to his. He runs his other hand down my body, feeling the curve of my breasts, my waist . . . I gulp in breath. He presses me up against the boat, his free hand grasping my hair. Against me, Nick's body is hard where mine is soft, and I almost groan aloud as his lips press against mine. I feel like I am part of him as I wrap my legs around his waist, only my thin silk panties between us. I suck on his lower lip, and he kisses up and down my neck, my back arching with the pleasure of it.

Then a wave crashes over both of our heads, and we

look up as a speedboat zips by, drenching us in its wake. The driver doesn't see us, but a blush spreads over my face anyway.

"We should probably go," I whisper.

"Just one more," Nick whispers back.

The last kiss is even better than the first.

Chapter Twenty

I DON'T KNOW HOW LONG we floated there, our bodies wrapped around each other, my heart melting into his until we were one being under the stars. Now, wearing my damp dress, with Mom's earring securely in my bra, I feel my cheeks blush with pleasure as I watch Nick's shadow on the water, rowing us to shore.

As we get closer to the dock, the smell of fish gets stronger. Above our heads, seagulls shriek as they fight for fish and a mariachi band strums five dueling guitars on the crowded dock. A line of vendors' voices compete with the guitars, their carts stacked high with sugar skulls and glossy clay skeletons.

When we pull up to the island, Nick ties the boat to the dock and jumps out, holding one hand out to me. I glance down at Paloma's mask, now wet and trampled on the bottom of the boat, and decide to leave it there. *I don't want to hide anymore*, I think as I take Nick's hand, never wanting to let go. A thought forms in my head: *Maybe I never have to.* Maybe I'll never go back to L.A. Maybe this could be the new me, this wet, dirty girl with a new name and a blank past. Maybe that wouldn't be so bad.

On the dock, my damp dress sticks to my body, and water pools in my sneakers. In front of us, hundreds of women carrying glowing lanterns climb the marble stairs up the island, disappearing into the darkness at the top. *That must be where the cemetery is.* To the right of the stairs, men in white clothing, with long braids hanging down their backs, are sitting at a small bar. They're watching a tiny black-and-white TV, which is shoved between two dusty bottles of tequila.

The dock is practically vacant by now, so I scan the guys at the bar for a man in a cowboy hat, but there's no one remotely close. Rapid pounding starts behind my ears. *What if Roberto left? What do I do then?* Sweat breaks out across my palms, but Nick just rubs his thumb over my skin in soft, soothing circles. *If Roberto never shows up, I can stay here with Nick, and we'll find someplace safe to hide. At least we'll be together.* I realize that I've never felt this whole with anyone before, so fully *me*—and I don't want this feeling to end.

My thoughts are interrupted as skeleton puppets as high as my waist bounce toward me, led by an old woman holding wooden sticks. *"¡Marionetas aquí!"* a voice croaks, stopping in front of me. From my other side, kids push packets of fluorescent gum into our hands and ladies thrust loaves of bread topped with ceramic doll heads at us. The sounds of their voices meld into one long cry. *"¡Pan de muerto a la venta! ¿Compre un Chiclet?"*

As they crowd closer, I get more nervous, my breath coming in quick, short gasps.

"Don't worry," Nick says, wrapping his arm around my waist. He mutters something in Spanish, and the vendors back away quickly, clearing a path.

With Nick by my side, I feel untouchable in a way I never have before. I glance at the shuttered white houses layered into the hillside and wonder what it would really be like to give up everything and stay here with Nick, never again hiding from the press, or avoiding the cameras on a bad hair day, or getting yelled at by a director for forgetting my lines. *Maybe Nick and I can live here forever, drinking out of coconuts and catching fish from the sea. I could be happy with that.* I'm trying to decide if I should spear the fish with sticks or catch them with my bare hands when I hear my name. And I don't mean Ines.

* * *

I glance at the TV on the bar just long enough to see my Oscar picture flashing across the screen. I duck my head, hoping Nick doesn't recognize me, but he's watching the crowd hike up the steep marble stairs.

Static shakes across the TV, and then another picture of me fills the screen: the grainy cell phone shot of my dead body in the apartment, a knife sticking through the back of my purple hoodie.

"Vivian Divine *no está muerta*," a reporter says.

On the screen, the reporter stands a few feet away from my body in the dirty apartment. Through the broken window, I can see police holding off a crowd in the street as the reporter continues, "*Y la revelación de una sorpresa . . .*"

Then a gloved hand reaches out and slowly turns the body over. It's my hair, my purple hoodie, but it's not me. *It's my body double. The actress who was in the hospital after the scaffolding collapsed under her.* I feel a rock sink down my chest and settle into a dull ache in my stomach. *But this time, she's really dead.*

I feel Nick's hand pulling on mine. "Let's go," he says, focused on the procession of women climbing the steps up the island. "People are leaving. They're opening the cemetery gates."

Take your eyes from the screen. Turn away. But I can't. Nothing in the world could distract me (not even the sexiest man alive breathing down my neck), because Pierre fills the screen. He's gesturing wildly with his hands, his eyes bloodshot.

"What's he saying?" I hear myself asking Nick.

Nick glances at the TV. "Some movie star was killed," he says, sounding bored by the topic, "and that kid claims he knows something, but he didn't say what."

I remember Pierre's words as I hung from the harness, and the words that he repeated later, when he tried to stop me outside my trailer: *Sparrow and I heard something strange. Something you should know.* I was so angry at the time that I barely heard his words. *But was he trying to tell me something? What did they hear that night?* After a microphone fumble, Pierre's face is replaced by Dad's. He's wearing a suit—not his normal boots and angel T-shirt, and he's actually *crying*.

It takes every bit of my strength to make my words sound casual. "What is he saying?"

"Her dad's begging anyone who's seen her to contact the number on the screen," Nick says, pointing to a ten-digit number scrolling across the bottom of the black-and-white TV. He's running his fingers through his hair, his eyes studying me intensely. "Why do you care?"

I tear my gaze away from the TV and look at him. *Can I afford to tell Nick the truth? Will that put him in more danger, or should he know the danger he's in, so he can protect himself?* I imagine a knife being plunged into Nick's back. *Wouldn't Nick be safer if he knew the truth, if he was ready to fight?* I glance around the empty dock, picturing Nick and I in the crosshairs of a gun. *Maybe it's time I tell Nick the truth about who I am—before he gets hurt.* I hold my hand out for him to take. "Can we go somewhere private?"

We find a quiet bench at the very end of the dock, where the tip of land meets the water. Once Nick finds out I lied to him, it's over. He trusted me, even risked his life for me, and I repaid him by lying to him about who I am? But by saving his life—am I ruining mine? I sit down on the bench and look out at the lake, stretching out the last few moments of bliss I have with him, because with me, when the truth comes out, it's never pretty. It's bloody, or obscured by yellow police tape, but it's never nice. *But maybe I'm not a very nice girl.*

I take a deep breath. "I have something to tell you," I begin, unable to look at him. "This is hard for me, but—"

"It was hard for me too," Nick says. *What the hell is he talking about?* "When I woke up on the road and you weren't there . . ." I think he's going to cry, but he rubs his fist in his eyes instead. "I thought someone had done something to you, something really bad, and I couldn't stand it, thinking that I could have protected you."

I want to stop him, I really do, but he's saying everything I want him to say. *How often does that happen?*

"I said I'm okay now," I say softly.

"Are you sure? Did someone . . . hurt you?"

I know the kind of hurt he means. The kind that rips a girl's soul out and leaves her empty.

"No," I say, "nothing like that." *Something else. Something that will drive you away from me, probably forever.* I suck in a breath and slowly let it out, trying to muster up all the courage I have. "That's what I want to talk to you about."

I'm hoping he'll distract me again, maybe even use the L-word. *But shouldn't Nick know the danger he's in, even if it means losing him forever?*

I start slowly, telling him almost everything: how a man forced me into his car but I got away, how Isabel protected me and took me into her home, how my real name is not Ines. It's actually kind of fun telling the story, like I'm writing a script "based on true events" that have nothing to do with me.

"But the priest was right, Nick," I finish, nearly out of breath. "Someone's trying to kill me."

"Who?"

"His name was Scars," I say. "He forced me into his car, and if we hadn't crashed, I'm sure he would've killed me."

Nick stares at me, the color draining out of his cheeks. He looks like he's been punched; his mouth hangs open, his wound shining like a branding mark on his rapidly graying face.

"Did you know him?" I ask.

"I know . . . of him." Nick's forehead is creased with tense wrinkles. He reaches out and rubs his trembling fingers softly across my cheek, traces the curve of my lips with his thumb. "If you're sure he was trying to kill you," Nick says, "we need to get you out of here, now."

"Now? But Scars is dead," I insist. "I'll be fine." *And if Marcos had Mom's earring, he might know who killed her. I have to find him, and find out the truth.* "I just need to go to—"

"No!" Nick grabs my hand and pulls me to my feet. "We need to get back to the boat now, and get you off this island."

"I'm okay now, remember? I'm with you."

"But I can't take care of you here," Nick says. He stares at the empty dock, where the last few people are now climbing the steps, leaving us alone. "I'll get you back to the mainland. You can hide for the night, and tomorrow we'll go north together." He pauses, his eyes suddenly narrowing.

"Nick? What is it?" I turn around, hoping to see Isabel hiking toward us, her smile containing questions that need answering. Or Roberto, my beacon of safety, pacing the dock in a cowboy hat, just like Mary promised he would be. But I don't see Isabel or Roberto on the vacant dock. Instead, there's a huge man walking toward us, a snake tattoo slithering up his face. Terror pins me to the bench.

How is he still alive? My throat closes up, and it feels like something's crushing my windpipe. *Scars couldn't have lived through that fire. Wasn't he stuck behind the wheel when the car exploded?*

"He's coming," I hiss, forcing the words out of my throat. *If we leave now, we can try to outrun him.* But before we can move, Scars is looming above us, his burned face a nest of squirming snakes.

Chapter Twenty-One

IF I SAID I'D SEEN the undead before now, I lied. The undead were always dressed in tacky clothes and dripping with fake blood. Their hands were shriveled into claws, and their masks molded into deadly screams. But even the best of Hollywood's undead couldn't have prepared me for this.

"Vivian," Scars growls, his gravelly voice rolling through me, pressing my feet into the ground. His green uniform is burned and torn, and some of the flesh has peeled off his face, leaving patches of raw red skin through his squirming snake tattoos. *He must have gotten out before the engine exploded.* I remember scrambling up the scalding rocks, my knees bleeding. *I outran him, but he didn't die.*

Scars glares at Nick with disgust, but when he shifts his gaze to me, he half smiles, which makes him even uglier than before. Scars pulls a gun out of his pocket, and I back away until my calves press into the bench behind me, desperately trying to think of an escape plan. *We can either jump into the water and swim until he shoots us in the back—or wait for him to shoot us here. Neither option is good.*

"Leave her alone," Nick says, stepping in front of me. He's at least six feet tall, but he still barely reaches Scars's shoulders.

Despite Scars's monstrous size, he's lightning fast. He shoves Nick into me, and I topple over the bench and slide to the ground. Scars reaches down and grabs me by the throat.

"Get away from her!" Nick lunges at him, but Scars's mouth just twists into a horrible, toothless grin. Then he cracks the side of Nick's head with his gun handle. Nick collapses, his body crumpling against the bench beside me.

"*Vamos,*" Scars says, pulling me so close I can smell the rancid scent of his burned skin. He shoves his gun into my side, and then he kicks Nick's limp body under the bench. "*Estúpido* Nicolas," he says.

I'm so shocked I barely notice Scars twisting my hands behind my back and maneuvering me across the dock. I hardly feel the gun poking into my spine, or the numbness flowing up my arms as he squeezes the circulation out of them. My mind is turning the same question over and over: *How did Scars know Nick's name?*

Before we join the end of the line of chanting women winding up the cemetery stairs, Scars pulls a skeleton mask out of his pocket and straps it on, hiding his horrifying face. I glance back, hoping Nick will chase after us, but I can barely see the tips of his shoes sticking out from beneath the wooden bench.

"Somebody help me," I whisper, but we're trailing far behind the women, and my words get lost in the hundreds of chanting voices above me.

On the long hike up the stairs, I can't stop thinking about Nick. *How did Scars know Nick's name? Did I yell it when he forced me into his car?*

From the top of the stairs, the cemetery gates are a short distance away. Lingering around the gates are ancient women with buckets of marigolds, little girls balancing stacks of spindly white candles, and a group of muscular men in white cotton, their braids dangling down to their knees.

"Where are you, Isabel?" I whisper. She was supposed to meet me at the entrance. *Did something happen to her?* The sting of salty tears burns in my eyes. *He's going to kill me in the cemetery and throw me in an open grave.*

But when we reach the cemetery gates, Scars makes an abrupt right, away from the graveyard. His hand tightens on my arm, and then he's marching me along the edge of the metal cemetery fence. Through the bars, I can see women in white dresses, their heads wrapped in gauzy shawls, wandering between the tombstones. I squint in the dim light, looking for Isabel, but I can't tell the features of anyone's faces in the hazy, incense-filled air. Orange flower petals line the outside of the fence in a wavy path, and I step on them as Scars yanks me along beside him. On the other side of the cemetery, where the fence ends, a white two-story house faces the graveyard. Behind the house, smaller white houses pile on top of each other down the hill, all the way to the lake.

I glance behind me, where the last of the women are pushing into the cemetery, and two of the men with long braids are now starting to close the gates. *I have to get away from Scars. But how? I can't fight him; he's too strong. And I can't scream, or he might shoot me.* I feel his hand tighten around my wrist. *You are stronger than you know*, I remember my mom telling me the day before she disappeared, when I was filming the fight scene for *Zombie Killer*. In that scene, when the zombies had me almost beaten, the Zombie Killer realized that sometimes *not* fighting is as powerful as fighting. *You are stronger than you know.*

I suddenly remember to relax all of the muscles in my body and drop limply to the ground. Scars's hand comes off my arm, and before he can grab it again, I jump up and sprint for the entrance. Scars bolts after me, but when I glance back, one of the long-braided men puts his hand against Scars's chest, stopping him in place.

"*No puede entrar*," I hear the man say.

Why did they stop Scars? Is evil not allowed in the graveyard? I dash through the gates, ducking into the procession of chanting women. *I don't really care why, as long as they keep him away from me.* Then the flower sellers follow me into the cemetery and, from the inside, lock the gates behind them. *Are they locking him out or locking me in?*

Behind me, Scars is yelling something in Spanish. When I glance back, the men are shoving Scars away from the gates, and he's lashing out like a dying fish. The old women surround me then, chanting softly, and I'm swept away with them into the glowing graveyard.

The cemetery is hazy with thick clouds of incense and fog rising from the lake. As I move deeper into the ghostly fog, relief flows over me, making me nearly limp. *I'm safe.* I'm instantly ashamed by my relief. *What about Nick? Is he okay?*

I want to turn around and go find him, but the crowd is too strong. I finally allow myself to be carried along, watching tombstones appear in the fog like apparitions and drop into nothing behind me. I'm dizzy with the smell of burning incense, rising in great gray puffs from every grave. *I need to find Isabel. She'll help me get to Nick.*

I weave through the candlelight, looking for Isabel and trying not to step on someone's grave. I'm suddenly grateful for my disguise: with my short black hair and white cotton dress, no one notices me. Only a few women glance up at me from the edge of the tombstones and smile; others ignore me, their eyes hazy as if they're looking into another world.

Finally, I see Isabel leaning back against a tombstone, one of her black braids draping over a small altar layered with apples and skull-shaped loaves of bread. Mounds of orange petals are piled up around her knees, like drifts of orange snow.

"Isabel?"

Isabel jumps up, a blizzard of flower petals cascading from her hands, and pulls me into a hug. "*Mi hija*, I was so worried. I waited at the entrance, but you never showed up. Then I came inside, thinking you would be in here, but I couldn't find you." I'm touched by how upset Isabel sounds. "Where were you?"

How do I even start to answer that question? *I was skinny-dipping in the lake after falling in love for the first time? Or I was being chased by a murderer I thought was dead? Or how about the worst one: I'm heartbroken because the murderer knew Nick's name, so the boy I fell in love with may be one of the men who is trying to kill me?*

"Did that boy hurt you?" Isabel asks.

"No," I say, choking up. "But I'm not sure I can trust him anymore."

"Why not?"

"The guy who forced me into his car is here," I say, my throat closing up so tightly I can barely breathe. "And he knew Nick, Isabel. He knew his *name*."

"So? Everyone knows everyone around here," Isabel says. "If you're not a cousin, you're a friend of a friend, or a friend of an enemy. Everyone knows each others' names."

"Even strangers?"

"*Sí*," Isabel says. "Even if you don't know someone personally, you've seen them, or know of them."

So that's how Scars knew Nick's name, the same way that Nick had heard of him. A cool feeling of relief fills my body. *How could I have ever doubted Nick? He risked his life for me—twice!*

As my throat loosens, allowing me to breathe again, I notice that the lines in Isabel's face are still tight with worry. "The man who forced you into his car," Isabel asks, "does he know where you are?"

I nod. "But those men wouldn't let him past the gates."

"On the Day of the Dead, no men are allowed into the cemetery until morning," Isabel explains. "Local tradition. The gates are locked, so no one goes in or out till sunrise. You'll be safe here tonight," she adds.

"But what about my friend?" *How could I leave him behind? He's probably injured, or worse.* "He's still at the dock. And he's hurt."

Isabel puts her hand on my shoulder. "Don't worry. If

he's at the dock, somebody will find him. *No te preocupes.*"

Nick's really tough, but he might be unconscious, bleeding to death all alone out there. "But I got him into this! I can't just do nothing."

"Your friend will be okay. Trust me," she coaxes, sitting back down beside the altar. "Besides, if that man knows where you are, you're the one in danger, not your friend." Isabel picks up a handful of orange petals and drops them onto the grave, filling in spots that are brown with dirt. "Now sit, and help me with the *cempasúchil.*"

Forcing myself not to imagine what's left of the body six feet below me, I perch lightly at the end of the grave. *She's right. Scars isn't after Nick, just me. He only hit Nick because he stood up for me. Maybe right now, the farther I am from him the better.* I grab a handful of orange petals and drop them gingerly, trying not to touch the dirt mound.

"She's not going to bite," Isabel says.

"Who?"

She points to an old black-and-white photo of a little girl on the altar. "My sister Aurora, Paloma's mom. She died two years ago, crossing to *el norte.*"

"So you buried her here?"

Isabel shakes her head. "They never found her body, but a lot of people drown, get covered by sand, even eaten by animals. So last year, I had a ceremony for her here, in secret. Even Marcos never knew."

The petals drop out of my hand and flutter down into the orange abyss. "Why would Marcos need to know?"

Isabel pulls a pack of matches out of her bag, lights one of the long white candles, and shoves it in the dirt at the edge of the grave. "Marcos owns the cemetery now," she says. "And everyone who is buried in it." Isabel pushes another candle into the dirt. She hands me the matches, and I light it, impatient to understand why I'm holding a handful of puzzle pieces that don't seem to make a puzzle. "See those stickers?" Isabel asks.

I look over at the nearest grave. There is a red-and-white sticker on the tombstone that says NICHO CADUCADO.

"Before Marcos bought the cemetery, those were the graves that were going to be dug up for not paying their leases," Isabel continues.

"Leases?"

"We can't buy gravesites here, so when someone dies, we rent one," Isabel says. "It's a small island, and there's only so many spaces. So every five years or so, we have to buy a new lease. When we can't afford it . . ." She makes a thumbs-up symbol and pops it into the air. "That's why the people love Marcos here," Isabel says, lighting another candle around the grave. "When Marcos got out of prison six months ago, he bought the cemetery, and now no one has to buy leases, and everyone's relatives get to stay in the ground."

"Why would he do that?"

Isabel lights the last candle, and there are now at least fifty white candles around Aurora's grave, each an inch apart in a long, glowing rectangle. "When he was in prison, they dug up his mother for not paying the lease," Isabel says. "He was so angry he bought the whole cemetery."

"So he's kind of a hero?"

"Kind of." Isabel bites her bottom lip nervously. "And kind of not."

POP! POP! POP!

I throw myself to the ground, cradling my head with my hands. My body spasms with fear, and I press myself harder into the dirt.

"Are you afraid of fireworks?" Isabel asks.

I timidly raise my head. Colors explode in bright handprints of light across the sky, crackling and sizzling as they cascade to the ground. I breathe in the smell of the loamy earth beneath me. Nobody's shooting at me; they're just fireworks.

Remember fun? Fourth of July? Those kinds of fireworks. I slowly uncurl myself from my spot on the ground and sit beside Isabel, my back resting uncomfortably against the side of Aurora's tombstone.

As the fireworks grow brighter, I see women across the cemetery taking out picnic baskets and unwrapping food from plastic bags. I'm suddenly starving. Beside me, Isabel rummages in her bag and then hands me a tamale wrapped in a cloth napkin. "Best tamales in Rosales, sold right outside these gates," she says.

I try to unwrap the tamale, but the tips of my fingers burn on the hot corn husk. "I love tamales," I say. "But they're just so fattening."

"You're tiny," Isabel says. "You can afford to gain a pound or two."

Now that's one I've never heard before. Between "the screen adds ten pounds" and "hello, fat; good-bye, career," I'm pretty much versed in the "less is more" mentality.

"You don't understand," I say, shaking my head. "If I get fat, I lose my career."

"Would that be so bad?"

I hesitate, my breath suspended in my throat and my fingers still burning on the steaming cornmeal. I imagine all the things I could do if I quit acting: eat ten tamales an hour. Go outside in my pajamas. Watch TV without cringing at my bad haircut. "I don't know," I whisper, "if anyone would love me without it."

Isabel takes my tamale and unwraps it so the cornmeal pokes out of the top, like a banana. When she hands it back to me, it's cool and sticky in my palm. "They would," Isabel says slowly. "But would you?"

It scares me that I don't know the answer.

All around me, children are poking fingers into their moms' pockets and pulling out long sticks, their tops wrapped in bundles of cloth. They light their crude sparklers, passing them from hand to hand. I feel a sharp tug on my hand as Isabel pulls me to my feet. The woman at the next grave hands Isabel two sticks, and she gives one to me, the bitter smell of gasoline filling my nostrils. We touch our gasoline-soaked tips to the woman's, and soon sparks are everywhere, bounding over graves, jumping the heads of tombstones.

I think about Marcos, and how he's a hero to the town, but I saw him burn a hole in his guard's hand for a simple mistake. *Who is he really? And why did he have my mom's earring?*

When the lights fade out of the sky, the women around us start gathering their bags. "Follow me, *mi hija*," Isabel says. She brushes the flower petals off my white dress, throws her bags over her shoulder, and grabs Abuelita's weaving. As she stands up, one end slips out of her hand, and the weaving unrolls, inch by inch, from her hands to the grave.

At first it looks like a mural of Mother Mary, like the one that's painted in the back lot's "Religious Italian Town" set. But something's a little off, so I step closer to Mother Mary's pale face. Beneath the blue headdress, and above her full lips, I see the hundred tiny weaves of my mother's heart-shaped mole, and hanging from her ears, identical pink roses.

For a moment I can't speak: my voice box has stopped

working. *Other than the blue headdress, it could be a photograph of Mom.* The ground shakes beneath my feet, dropping my stomach and weakening my knees.

"What's wrong?" Isabel asks.

I realize I've moved closer to the rug, until my nose almost touches the soft wool. "That's my mother."

Isabel beams at me like I said the right answer to a long-unanswered question. "She's everyone's mother."

"No, it's not Mother Mary," I insist, shaking my head. "It's my mom. Pearl Divine."

"The movie star?" Isabel asks, looking at it closely. "Are you sure?"

I nod. "Those are her earrings," I say, "and her mole." Both years Mom was voted Sexiest Woman in Hollywood, the press focused on her heart-shaped mole, which Dad swore was an imprint of the first kiss he ever gave her. "How did Abuelita know what my mom looked like?" I demand.

"Abuelita just weaves whatever she's asked to," Isabel says. "This must have been the picture Marcos brought over."

"But—"

"I know how much it hurts," Isabel says gently. "But your mother's gone, Vivian. And even finding out what happened to her won't bring her back."

I grate my teeth into my skull and clench my fists by

my side. "Maybe not. But I need to know why Marcos had Mom's earring, and why he paid Abuelita to weave her portrait," I say, pressing my finger into the weaving. "I have to know the truth."

"And what if the truth is that he killed her?"

"Then I'll kill him," I growl. "And that'll make the pain stop."

Isabel puts her hand on my shoulder. I want to shake it off, tell her I don't need any pity, but I let it rest there instead, like a weight holding me in this world. "The pain does stop, *mi hija*, but not through hurting someone else. And not all at once. Over time, it just slowly fades away."

I want to believe that, but every morning, I wake up hoping to see Mom's face, and every morning, her absence hurts more than it did the day before. "For me," I say, "the pain just gets worse."

"That's because it's different for everyone," Isabel says. "I mourned for different amounts of time for my mom, my dad, my sister. Some losses are easier to live with, and some stay around longer."

"What do you mean?"

Isabel studies me for a second. "Did you ever get hurt, get cut or something?"

Like being thrown from a horse? I nod.

"Grief is like that. It starts off as a painful, bloody wound, then it crusts into a scab, and eventually, it fades into a scar," Isabel says. "The scar's always there, but it doesn't hurt anymore."

"So one day," I say, taking a deep breath. "The pain ends?"

"It ends. And then you know you can live through anything, so you stop being so afraid."

"Of what?"

"Of everything," Isabel says. "We fear what we think we can't handle. If you can handle this, you can handle anything."

Isabel's words make me feel calm inside for the first time since Mom died. *I can handle this. I can go on, be less afraid.* I feel my muscles relax, my jaw unclench, my heartbeat slow. Someday, I won't feel like every day is crushing me into little bits.

There's something comforting about knowing that one day the pain ends, and you get stronger, until you can handle whatever comes your way. *Maybe Mom was right.* I watch the last of the fireworks sizzle to the ground, spiraling blue, green, and red lights across the white tombstones. *Maybe I am stronger than I think.*

I nod at Isabel. "Let's go," I say, grabbing the weaving off the ground. *Maybe I do have the courage to keep going, to find out what happened to Mom.*

Chapter Twenty-Two

THE SUN IS JUST TIPPING its head over the lake when we reach the church at the end of the cemetery. A ghostly fog hangs over the building, obscuring the procession of mourners winding through the thick stone doorway.

The church looks like it's straight out of *The Hunchback of Notre-Dame*, with its spindly spires and stone dark enough to have been roasted in a fire. On the steeple, a small boy is hanging from the heavy iron bell, posed as if about to ring it. *Or jump off the building.*

"Does anybody ever—"

"Jump?" Isabel answers. "Just last year. A man betrayed la Familia de Muerta, so he took a nose-dive into the center of the square. But I wouldn't say *jumped* is the right word. More like *pushed.*"

I remember the cut on the little girl's face, and how she said it was la Familia de Muerta that did it, and how I held my hand over my heart to translate the word *Nick* to her, before I even knew I loved him. I try to shake him out of my mind. I don't want to think about Nick, where he is, if someone found him under that bench. I remember him taking off his shirt, the muscles in his arms as he held me in the lake, his mischievous smile, that wound on his forehead . . .

Stop thinking! I try to focus on the men and women now filtering through the giant gold doors into the church, skeleton masks hiding their eyes, but I can't. I'm too distracted by thoughts of Nick. *But the farther Nick is from me, the better off he is. I can give him that much, for now.* I watch people taking skeleton masks from a man standing near the door, and strapping them on as they enter the church. I take one too and strap it over my eyes.

My stomach is violently twisting and turning as we get closer to the entrance. *What if Marcos just bought the earring, and he doesn't know anything about Mom's disappearance? If so, then why does he have a weaving of her face?* I pause in front of the church doors, wondering if it's too late to bolt down the stairs and catch the nearest boat home. *And if he didn't buy the earring, could Marcos have been involved in Mom's murder?* I force myself to take a deep breath and straighten my shoulders. *If Mom were this close to finding out what happened to me, she wouldn't back out*, I say to myself as I push through the thick gold doors behind Isabel.

Compared to the small cemetery, the church is enormous. Above me, a glass dome scatters light across the rows of red velvet pews, and the sunrise peeks through the stained glass window above the altar.

It looks like a normal church overall, except for the altar, which has been transformed into a stage set, complete with a fifteenth-century plastic graveyard. It's not as fancy as the studio's graveyard set, but the story's the same: Don Juan, a cheating scumbag, kidnaps his fiancée, Ines, and kills her father. Ines dies of sorrow, but then she forgives Don Juan for his sins and pulls him up to heaven. *What fool would forgive him for that?*

In front of the altar, people are flocking to Marcos, who is standing royally by the first pew with an indulgent smile. Women approach him shyly and kiss his hands, and men in grubby white clothes openly admire his red silk suit. Little kids dash around his feet, and he picks them up and tickles them, their laughter filling the church.

"What's going on?" I ask Isabel as a boy clip-clops up to Marcos on shiny steel crutches. Marcos kneels down and ruffles the kid's hair.

"Marcos paid for that boy's crutches," Isabel says. "The

people ask him for favors, and he never refuses: he buys the cemetery to save our ancestors, gets crutches for injured kids, delivers sacks of apples for Los Muertos . . ." She rolls her eyes. "People love him around here."

"What about you?"

Isabel shrugs. "He always shows up smiling at the charity events he gives. But when Aurora worked for him, he would make her do horrible things to people." She shudders. "Things no good person would do."

"But he seems so—"

"I know," she says. "Just wait here. I'll go find out what Marcos knows, before I lose my nerve."

With the weaving tucked under one arm, Isabel hurries through the crowd, passing the red velvet pews, which are filling up with people wearing skeleton masks.

When Marcos sees Isabel, he kisses her politely on the cheek and takes the weaving. He immediately unrolls it, and I wince as I get a flash of Mom's heart-shaped mole. Marcos nods, looking pleased, and then Isabel leans in and whispers something to him. Angry lines harden on Marcos's face as he answers back, and I suddenly notice how his red silk suit, the same color as the pews, glimmers like a wet bloodstain.

After he finishes talking, Isabel heads back up the aisle, joining me beside the last pew. "I asked Marcos if he was pleased with the weaving of Mother Mary, and if not, he could have a new one *gratis*," Isabel says. "Marcos said it wasn't Mother Mary, but he accepted the free weaving anyway."

"Then who is it?" I hold my breath, waiting to hear the two words I've been praying for: Pearl Divine.

"I don't know." The bell booms through the church, shaking the floor beneath me. "But there's nothing more I can do. I'm sorry."

I can tell she means it, and I'm sorry too—for putting her through all of this. *Maybe I'm making this all up, and Mom's earring really was stolen, and Marcos bought the weaving of Mom because he's just one of the million Pearl Divine fans.* I watch the crowd, in their creepy skeleton masks, as everyone finds a place to stand or sit, while the bell rings once, twice, three times.

When the last bell rings with a resounding clang, Marcos stands up in the front pew. He walks toward the stage, his foot dragging slightly behind him, and the tapping of his cane seems almost as loud as the last clanging of the bell.

As Marcos climbs onto the stage, people drop into silence, all at once, like a lid closing on a coffin. Standing alone onstage, he looks like one of those televangelists, too good-looking to be holy, too slick to be honest.

"*Bienvenidos, amigos. Tengo una mala noticia,*" he says. "*El primer actor sufrió un accidente.*"

"What's he saying?" I whisper in Isabel's ear.

"He says the lead actor had an accident," she translates, but by the way she says *accident*, I can tell there was nothing accidental about it.

I turn my attention back to Marcos, but the only word I can understand out of his speech is *amo*: I love. I remember when someone spray painted that word on the studio gate, with the letter *I* above it, and even after the janitors painted over it, I could still see the words: "I love." If I were to write that now, I'd put the word *Nick* after it.

"Marcos says the person standing in for the lead actor is someone very dear to him; his *ahijado*," Isabel says. "His godson."

A man stands up in the second pew and walks up to Marcos, his back to the crowd. Marcos put his arm around the actor's shoulders, and then turns him to face the audience. "*Mi ahijado*, Nicolas."

Chapter Twenty-Three

MY HEART SHATTERS INSIDE my chest.

The broken pieces of whatever love I had left cut me up inside. I want to curl up, to protect myself, but it's too late. I'm already bleeding inside. My face gets hot with shame when I think about all the private things I told him. I've never felt so stupid, so betrayed, so completely worthless. *How did I not see this before? The gun he carried for "protection," the "shipping company" he worked for, his godfather going to prison for "tax evasion"? Nobody goes to prison for fifteen years for tax evasion!*

Standing beside Marcos, Nick has a hard, cold look on his face, the same look he had when he ordered the Zapotec boy in the cowboy hat to stop calling me the White

Devil. *Was that what the kid was really saying? Or was he trying to tell me the danger I was in?*

I squeeze my eyes shut so tightly I see white squiggly lines float behind my eyelids, willing it to be different when they open.

It isn't.

Nick's still standing up there, addressing the crowd in Spanish. He looks exactly the same as he did when I fell in love with him, except he's wearing the same green uniform Scars was wearing when he returned from the dead. *Was Nick planning to hand me over to Scars? Is that why he met me at the dock? And did Scars even hit Nick, or was that all pretend, too?*

My whole body flushes with shame and hurt. Our kisses, our naked swim, me sleeping in his arms? I thought he was falling in love with me. *Was he just using me the whole time?*

Of course he was. My blood starts to boil with anger. At first it's just a little bubble, but it quickly turns into a steaming, overflowing pot of rage. I think I'm going to burst out of my skin. *I'm so stupid! How could I have ever believed he cared about me?*

"I hate him," I whisper as Nick walks upstage and disappears behind the curtain.

Isabel looks at me in surprise. Before she can ask me anything, however, Marcos steps off the stage and the lights drop.

When Nick comes back onstage wearing the mask of

Don Juan, I grind my teeth until my jaw hurts. I think about all the times Nick humiliated me, how he made me fall in love with him, how he pretended to fall in love with me.

Isabel grabs my hand. "Is something wrong?"

"That's him," I mutter, rage burning through me, pushing out sweat through every gland. *The boy I fell in love with. The boy I gave my heart to, who told me I could trust him with it. The boy who lied to me.*

During Act One's first big scene, where Don Juan kidnaps his fiancée, Ines, I rack my brain for reasons Nick would pretend to care about me. *But the chemistry was real, wasn't it? Or did he have orders to pretend to care about me, just to deliver me to his godfather? If so, what does Marcos want with me?*

During the second part of Act One where Don Juan kills Ines's father, I remember how Nick told me how he woke up on the side of the road, practically unharmed. *How could I have missed it? Of course Scars didn't hurt his boss's godson! But then why did Nick try to protect me from Scars at the dock, and why did Scars hit him with his gun?* The answer works itself out: That was an act, all planned beforehand. All the pieces fall into place, and my hate toward Nick turns into something else: revenge.

During Act One's finale, where Don Juan flees the country, leaving Ines to die of sorrow, I'm concocting a dozen ways I can make Nick pay (boiling oil? ripping out his fingernails?) when I hear a familiar voice. I'm not sure where it's coming from, and it's so soft I'm not sure I heard it at all. But it reminds me of bright red lipstick and kisses before bed. Tears spring to my eyes and my ears ache to hear that familiar voice again:

Mom's voice.

Chapter Twenty-Four

BY THE TIME THE LIGHTS go on for intermission, I've convinced myself it was Mom's voice I heard. *It had to be.* Then again, there's no other voice in the world I want to hear more, so I must have imagined it. *But what if I didn't?*

"Where's the dressing room?" I ask Isabel, looking at the empty stage.

"Behind the altar," Isabel says. "Why?"

"This is going to sound crazy, but I think I heard my mom's voice."

Isabel looks at me like I've lost my mind. "Are you sure?"

"Not at all. But Marcos has to be involved in this," I say, thinking of Mom's earring and the weaving of her face. *It all leads back to Marcos.* "I think the voice was coming from backstage," I explain, feeling crazier every second. *Don't do this to yourself. She's gone, like Isabel said.* But I can't stop myself. "Will you help me?"

"What do you think?" Isabel sighs, and I see that maybe I'm not just a stand-in for her dead niece. Maybe she cares about me—for me. I feel my eyes tear up. "I'll distract him," Isabel continues. "You have two minutes to get to the dressing room."

I don't know how to thank her. Nobody's ever risked their life for me—unless they were getting paid to.

"Thanks for—"

"Later," she says. "You better get moving."

It takes me a total of thirty seconds to bolt through the crowd into the alcove left of the altar. *I just need to get across the altar and through the curtain. After that, I'll just sneak backstage and hope I hear that voice again. Easy.* I glance over at Marcos sitting in the first pew, his eyes on the stage. *But where is Scars? And how will I get across the stage without Marcos seeing me?*

Isabel suddenly pushes over a pew, and a thunderous bang echoes through the church. Marcos flips around in his seat, but Isabel has already disappeared into the crowd.

This is my chance: I run for it.

I dash across the stage, expecting to shock Nick by showing up in his dressing room. *This totally isn't worth it. I probably just imagined her voice.* Imagining myself stuck alone on the stage, I sprint to the small door behind the altar, rip it open, and shut it behind me.

The room behind the altar is set up as a miniature dressing room: mirrors with round bulbs, makeup in boxes on the dressing tables, wigs and costumes hanging in movable plastic closets. *But no one's here.* I feel my heart sink. *Then where was that voice coming from?*

I catch sight of myself in the mirror, realizing that this is the first mirror I've seen in days. For a girl who's lived her entire life in front of a mirror, and tracked every tiny change in skin appearance and weight gain with meticulous concern, I'm surprised I didn't notice it missing before, aching like a phantom limb. Glancing at my reflection again, I can't believe how much I've changed in a few days. My chopped black hair is oily and stringy, and Paloma's white cotton dress hangs off me in loose white folds. My skin is tanned from the last four days in the sun, and my lips are chapped from the wind.

In fact, the last time I saw myself in a mirror was the night Nick and I stayed at his cousin's house. My chest aches from Nick's betrayal, and there's this itchy feeling under my skin reminding me that I don't know who to trust anymore. *Was it even his cousin's house, or was that a setup too?* I want to scream, to set fire to this place that made me imagine Mom's voice, but I can't, because the door to the dressing room opens, and a chill bolts up my spine.

The girl who shuffles into the room, her shoulders slumped over her thin chest, looks like she was beautiful once. Now, her ragged black hair hangs over her face, like a dark veil, and her eyes trail the ground as she walks. She's otherworldly, ethereal, like a ghost who's come home for the Day of the Dead.

The girl shuffles past me, hardly noticing me, and starts rearranging brushes on the dressing room table. I'm standing frozen behind her, watching her line up the lipsticks.

"Who are you?" I whisper.

I'm afraid she's going to scream or strike out at me, but there's no reaction in her face at all. She just drops a burgundy-colored lipstick. It rolls across the floor to my feet, and when I pick it up, the name printed across the bottom is mom's favorite: Tango Red.

"*Me llamo?*" she says. Her voice is so monotone it's chilling, as if all the expression has been beaten out of it. I notice that the skin around her left eye is bruised, and her nails are chewed to short, ragged edges.

"I'm . . . I'm Vivian," I stutter. "Do you speak English?"

"A *leetle*," she says. The girl's eyes grow narrow, suspicious, and she glances around the room as if there's a ghost in here with us. "*Me llamo* Paloma."

My heart catches in my chest. *Isabel's Paloma? Her missing niece? Is it possible that she's still alive?* I study her face in the dim light of the dressing room. She *does* look like the girl in the weaving above Paloma's altar, except a lot skinnier and paler. *Why would she lie? But if it is her, why would she be back here, in this creepy dressing room, at a play Marcos is putting on?* I feel my heartbeat thump once, twice, before I trust myself to speak.

"Paloma?" I ask softly.

Tears well up in her eyes as if nobody's said her name in years. Then she nods, her black hair dangling in her face, covering her bruised eye.

"*¿Este vestido?*" she asks, reaching out to rub the end of my rough cotton dress between her fingers. "Is mine?"

I look down at the ratty, once-white dress Isabel lent me, and nod. It's definitely had better days. Covered in dirt from the cemetery, it looks like a dead animal the dog dug up. "From Isabel."

Paloma looks confused that I know Isabel, but she doesn't speak much English, and I don't know enough Spanish to explain how Marcos had Mom's diamond earring, and how I heard a voice coming from backstage that sounded like my mom's, so I just point to my eyes, and say, "Have you seen Pearl Divine?"

Paloma doesn't answer; she just bites on her lip so hard I'm sure blood's going to spout from it any second. "*No he visto.*" She shakes her head, tears gathering like storm clouds in her eyes, and adds, "No talk."

"No talk?" I repeat.

Paloma clamps her hand over her mouth as if she's said too much, and my whole body starts tingling. *I know she's hiding something, but how can I find out what it is?* I remember what Mary once said: *The secret to getting what you want is having what they need.* I point to her, and say: "If you talk . . ." I crook my index finger in a come-here gesture, and say, "I'll take you with me"—I point to my eye—"to see Isabel."

For a brief second, Paloma lights up like a flame that's been hidden for too long. *She's going to tell me!* Then she lifts my hand and places it on her cheek. Under my unwilling fingers, I feel a hard mound of skin, half an inch wide. With her hand on top of mine, I follow the hard bulge down her cheek to the bottom of her chin.

"I talk," she says.

First the little girl, now Paloma? Did Scars cut her face too? Before I can ask her who did that to her, I hear footsteps on the other side of the door. "Tell me what you know about Pearl Divine," I plead, dropping my voice to a whisper.

"*Siga los cempasúchiles,*" Paloma whispers.

What?

The door opens. I hear dialogue coming from the stage, and then Scars's huge body fills the doorway. "Vivian," he growls, and steps into the dressing room, closing the door behind him.

I retreat farther into the room, but Scars keeps moving closer, until I'm backed up against the dressing room mirror. I see Paloma's terrified eyes beside me, and then a glint of metal shimmers through the air in front of my face. Within seconds, it's inches from my cheek, and I see my unscarred skin reflected in the knife's thin blade. My horrified look stares back at me: eyes wide, mouth gaping open, cheeks soft and smooth. Scars pushes the blade closer to my face, and I feel the edge of the knife, thin as a paper cut, across my cheek. I hear Mom's words in my head: *You're stronger than you know.* And I think, *Maybe she's right. Maybe I can save myself.*

It happens like this:

I slam my knee between his legs.

The knife clatters to the floor.

Paloma gasps.

I shove the door open and burst onto the stage.

Everything stops.

The audience cranes their rapt faces away from the final death scene, where Nick, dressed as Don Juan, is standing with one foot in the grave, stuck between heaven and hell. He stares at me, frozen in place. I glare back, hoping my look is burning a hole through his heart.

"*Toma de la mano,*" the actress says, leaning off the tombstone and extending her hand to him. Nick doesn't move, but his eyes shift slightly to the right as Scars lands behind me on the stage. I try to run, but I can't make my legs work.

I feel like I'm in one of those slow-motion dreams where you're running as fast as you can but you're not going anywhere.

"*¡Toma de la mano!*" the actress repeats, her voice high and whiney. She leans down and grabs Nick's hand.

Nick shakes her off and points behind me. "Watch out!" he yells. His voice jolts me into action, and I jump off the stage, Scars and his cheek-carving blade inches behind me.

As soon as I hit the ground, the crowd explodes in chaos. Pews scrape across the floor as people jump up, shuffling into each other. Kids wail in confusion, and Spanish phrases are fired like stray bullets:

"*¿Qué pasa? ¿Quién es ella?*"

Pain sears through my skull as Scars grabs a fistful of my hair and yanks me off my feet. *He's not going to let go.* I try to get to my feet but the burning in my scalp pulls me back down. *He's going to kill me here, in front of all these people.* But then, in the front pew, Marcos rises to his feet and shakes his head at Scars.

"*No aquí,*" Marcos says under his breath.

Scars abruptly lets go of my hair, and I stumble onto my feet, my scalp stinging. *Why is Marcos trying to help me?* I force Marcos out of my mind and focus on the crowd, which is parting as I push my way to the gold doors, to freedom.

"Try to run," Marcos calls, his voice echoing in the massive church chamber. I glance back at him as he surveys the crowd, and then he looks smugly at me and says: "Just try to run, Vivian Divine."

How does Marcos know my name? Confusion swims through my head as his words slap the crowd into a stunned silence. *Does he recognize me from TV, despite my disguise?* I feel my legs tremble beneath me as the silence turns to whispers, and then I hear it, what I've heard all my life. Person to person, voice after voice, it's whispered: *Vivian Divine. Vivian Divine.*

All heads turn toward me, one by one. Other than Marcos and me, most of the crowd's wearing skeleton masks, their grins fleshless and maniacal. The whispers circle around my head, folding people toward me.

"*La actriz . . .*"

"*Está muerta . . .*"

"Vivian Divine . . ."

Oh God. Not here. I scramble toward the doors, but it's too late. The crowd closes in around me, shoving up against my body until they're all I can see.

"Hollywood?" one woman yells. "Hollywood?" She grabs at my clothes, a familiar hunger in her eyes. I throw myself against the crowd, but they've become a wall: I can't get out.

I'm locked in by my own fame.

Bodies are pressing against mine, and hands are touching me from every direction, curious about my clothes, my hair, my skin. I'm suffocating, shrinking into the fetal position, my hands wrapped around my head. *I'm going to die right here.*

Then, in the sea of people, there's a hand reaching toward me. *Isabel.*

"*Niña,* now!" I grab onto her hand and let it tow me through the crowd. When we reach the door, Isabel crouches down, her face still covered by her skull mask, and lifts a metal rod out of a hole in the floor. "*¡Vamos!*" she says, pushing the door open, one hand still clamped tightly around the metal rod.

I grab on to her other hand and we race out of the church together. Yellow explodes behind my eyes as sunlight drenches me in its blinding light. When my sight clears, the cemetery doesn't look as scary now—or as magical. Wax has solidified in distorted droplets on burned-out candles, and the orange marigold petals are wilting to a light brown on the graves.

Now we need to get off this island, and fast. The sooner we get out of here, the sooner we can get help for Paloma. I watch Isabel shove the metal rod between the two door handles, locking the church from the outside. On the locked doors, the carvings of the mangled people in hell, burning in gold flames, flicker in the bright morning light. I can almost hear them screaming.

"Isabel," I say. "Paloma—"

"Later."

We're rushing through the cemetery, our shoes slapping the marble tips of graves, when Isabel trips. She lands hard on her knee and collapses onto a flower-strewn grave, the ribbons in her braids spiraling out behind her skeleton-masked face like red sun rays.

I wrench her to her feet and sling her arm around my shoulders. With Isabel groaning at every step, we limp to the end of the graveyard. Outside the gates, the white marble stairs are nearly blinding in the direct sunlight. I shield my eyes with my hand, and I notice a figure standing at the top of the stairs. *Probably a flower seller peddling her last wares.*

When we finally reach the gate, the bright sun is slipping behind the clouds. The blinding reflection from the stairs is fading, revealing the space between the gate and the white marble stairs, and I can see the figure on the top step more clearly now. She's wearing a traditional white dress, her hair plaited into a long braid. *It's not a flower seller.* I grab the tall iron gate, suddenly feeling protected again.

It's Mary.

She's here to rescue me.

Only Mary could find me out here, in the middle of nowhere. *Did she bring the CIA? The army? Dad's security team?*

Joy pulses through me. *Everything's going to be okay.* I don't know how she found me, but I don't care. *We're going home!*

I look around, expecting masked men to drop from heli-copters, their guns drawn. *Any moment now.*

"Mary!" I call, but she just glances at me, and then flicks her eyes away. *She's telling me to stay quiet.* I drop my hands from the gate, hoping to fade into the shadows until Mary reveals her plan to get me out of here. I'm scanning the horizon for snipers' rifles or police helmets when I notice Isabel standing stock-still beside me. She's staring at Mary, her fingers clenched so tightly around the gate that veins are standing up on the backs of her hands.

Then from out of nowhere, another figure appears at the top of the stairs, his red suit a shimmering spot on the blue horizon. *Marcos.* I shrink back from the gate. *Where did he come from? And how did he get here so fast?*

A vein pops out in Mary's forehead. *"Dónde está mi hija?"*

Marcos steps closer to her, so that they're facing each other at the top of the stairs, their dark figures encased by bright light. "Welcome to Rosales," he says, stepping for-ward to give her a kiss on the cheek, but Mary turns her face away.

"Hola, Marcos," she says stiffly.

"Hable inglés," Marcos says. "I want Vivian to hear this."

Dread wraps through my body, blurring my vision and making my hands tremble. *Even if Marcos has seen me on TV, what could he possibly want me to hear?*

"Okay, *señor,*" Mary says. "No more games. Just hand

her over." Nobody can resist Mary's demands. Not studio execs, or producers, or directors with tight schedules. And neither can Marcos, apparently.

"If it means that much to you," Marcos says, "you can have her."

I knew she'd come for me! The gate scrapes along the ground as I push it open and step through. *I'm here, Mary! I'm coming!*

Then something cinches around my waist, locking me in place. I fight against the huge arm, squirming with snake tattoos as it wraps tightly around my body. In Scars's other arm, Paloma struggles to pull out of his grip. "Mary!" I yell, but she keeps beaming at me with a stupid, dreamy grin.

"Paloma!" Isabel shrieks, and then Scars shoves Paloma, and she stumbles across the dirt patch toward the staircase, landing on the ground at Mary's feet.

Mary gazes down, and she doesn't seem to notice me screaming from the gate twenty feet away. She looks so happy: in her panicked state, she must think Paloma's me. But then Mary lifts Paloma's face up to hers and says, "Palomita. My baby girl."

Chapter Twenty-Five

HOW DOES MARY KNOW PALOMA? A million tiny needles pierce my skin, and then a ringing starts in my head. I unconsciously tighten my fist, squeezing Scars's hand like I used to squeeze Mary's when I was nervous. Scars glances at me in irritation, and squeezes back until the blood starts draining from my arm. *What the hell is going on?*

I feel like I'm looking at one of those superimposed photos, the kind where one person's face is pasted onto another person's body. And besides the fact that the girl in Mary's arms should be *me*, not Paloma, there's something strange about Mary. Her hair is pulled back into a braid, and she's wearing a white cotton dress. *What happened to her black uniform?*

"Palomita," Mary says, crouching down beside Paloma and cupping her cheek in her palm. Paloma tries to pull away, but Mary holds her close. Paloma doesn't look scared, exactly, like reporters look when Mary shields me from them; just hesitant, and angry.

"Not the welcome home you expected, Aurora?" Marcos asks.

Aurora. Suddenly, I feel tingling up and down my arms, like when you're spinning too fast and the tips of your fingers feel like they're tearing off. The ringing in my head increases, until it's a solid buzz. *Paloma's mother?* For a long moment, I can't breathe. *Mary is Isabel's dead sister?* That's not possible! She's *my* Mary. For the past two years, she's taken me to every rehearsal, film shoot, interview, wrap party. She was happy for me when I met Pierre, and hated him for me when he betrayed me. *She can't be Aurora!* I remember the nights that Mary sat by my side after Mom died, and how she always comforted me when I woke up screaming from a nightmare. Besides, Isabel said that Aurora died crossing the border two years ago. *But her body was never found.*

I yank my arms forward, but Scars's grasp is too tight, and my elbows feel like they're being pulled out of their sockets. *I thought Mary and I knew everything about each other! Or maybe she just knew everything about me.*

Beside me, Isabel is holding on to the iron gate, her hands trembling, her mouth gaping in disbelief. "Aurora?"

"Shut up, Isabel!" Mary hisses, and then returns to

caressing Paloma's terrified face. Paloma scoots away from Mary, using her feet to propel her backward. "¡Me abandanó!" Paloma shrieks.

Mary grabs onto one of Paloma's ankles before she slips out of reach, and reels Paloma back toward her. Paloma scrambles to grab the ground, but Mary's too strong. She pulls Paloma close and wraps her arms around her in a tight hug. "Mi hija," Mary says.

Paloma shakes her head furiously, trying to pry Mary's hands off her skinny body. "¡Me abandanó!" she screams again.

"English, ladies," Marcos interrupts, leaning all of his weight on his good leg and swinging his cane in a slow circle. "We've got a distinguished guest."

Paloma breaks out of Mary's grasp and runs across the dusty ground between the white marble stairs and the cemetery gate. She throws herself into Isabel's arms and bursts into tears.

"You *abandoned* her, Aurora," Isabel says to Mary. "It's been *two years.*"

"That doesn't matter," Mary says through gritted teeth. I remember how Mary clenches her jaw at night, and how she said it was because she was worried all day about me. *It was never me she was worried about—that was all a lie.* "She's *my* daughter!" Mary yells at Isabel, her eyes filled with rage.

Isabel cradles Paloma to her side, and her gentleness is

gone. She's fierce, a warrior. "This is Paloma's choice," she says, and turns to Paloma. "*¿Tu madre o yo?*"

Paloma looks back and forth between them, her lips quivering with indecision, but then she hugs Isabel tighter, hiding her face in Isabel's purple dress.

"But *I'm* her mother," Mary says, her face filling up with red until it looks like an overripe plum. "Tell Isabel to give her back!" she screams at Marcos.

Marcos swings his cane in a lazy circle. "This has nothing to do with me," he says.

"But you promised to give me Paloma," Mary says, her fists squeezing into rocks by her sides. "If I gave you Vivian."

The bottom of my heart drops out. I actually feel it hit the ground, roll around in the dust, and break open. *Mary gave me away to some psycho who might have killed my mom and probably wants to kill me, too?* As I struggle against Scars's grip, my mind spins back through the two years Mary's spent by my side: how she knew where to park the limo so the press couldn't see me, how she learned every word of Pierre's song about me so we could sing it together, how she guarded me against the press and Pierre's betrayal, and how she knew everything about me, even the ugly parts. *It was her job*, I realize. Hurt like a bullet slices into me, exploding in my stomach and tearing apart my insides. *She never really loved me.*

"How could you do this to me?" I yell, ripping out of

Scars's grip and charging toward Mary. Scars lunges after me, but Marcos shakes his head, and Scars stops in place. "I trusted you!"

Mary's arms shoot out and grip my wrists with the kind of force I've seen her use to wrench journalists from my window. "I had to, V. He had my daughter."

"But you said you loved me!"

"I do love you, but I love my daughter more," Mary says, tears streaming down her cheeks. She slightly relaxes her grip on my wrists, but not enough for me to pull away. "I wish it didn't have to be this way," Mary continues. "I wish I could take it back."

"Which part do you wish you could take back?"

"All of it. Leaving my daughter, accepting the job as your bodyguard, helping Marcos kidnap Pearl, fooling you into coming down here."

I suddenly feel like I'm in a sandstorm; my skin is stinging and hot tears are burning my eyes. I try to blink them away, but I can't stop them from streaming down my face. "Then why did you do it?" I cry.

"You know why," Mary says. She lets go of my wrists, and my arms drop limply to my sides. She turns toward Paloma, and, hovering by the gate twenty feet away, Isabel pulls Paloma tighter into her arms. "I never wanted to leave Paloma," Mary says to Isabel. "But Marcos asked me to watch over Vivian until he got out of prison. He promised he'd pay me more money than I'd ever seen. I . . . I thought it was only for a year and then I'd come home with money that could change our lives! But he said I couldn't bring Paloma with me, or tell you what I was doing. It wasn't safe."

It wasn't safe? With the back of my hand, I rub the tears off my face so hard it feels like I'm tearing through my skin. *What about my safety?*

Mary turns and glares at Marcos. "But when you got out of prison, you didn't pay me. You kidnapped Paloma instead, so I had to do what you told me to. And it was always one more thing: Just kill a Pearl Divine impersonator, you said," Mary seethes, her voice full of venom. "Bring me Pearl, you said, and then you'd give Paloma back. But you didn't. Liar!" she yells.

Marcos lifts his eyebrows, tempting her to say more.

Mary shakes her head angrily, the vein in her right temple throbbing, and then she shifts her gaze back to me. "He wouldn't give Paloma back—not until I delivered you to him. And with Mr. Divine's added security, kidnapping wasn't an option."

"How could you?" I demand, pressing so close to Mary that she has to back up to keep standing.

"I didn't have a choice. He would have killed my *daughter*," Mary says, her eyes teeming with tears. "And he arranged everything. I just had to be at the right place, at the right time. And it wasn't hard," she adds. "All it took was a cheap video, a fake DNA test, and an easily fooled body double. Everything can be bought, you know, with the right funds."

I don't realize that I am backing up in horror, but there's suddenly a large distance between Mary and me. My fists are squeezed into tight balls, wanting to pummel her until she feels the pain I'm feeling right now, but at the same time, my legs are yelling for me to run as fast as I can away from her.

"So that's it?" I snap. "It was that easy?"

"Well, it did get complicated at the end." Mary shakes her head. "Sparrow and Pierre almost ruined it when they saw that FBI agent threatening me," she says. "Pierre tried so hard to warn you, and if he had, my Palomita wouldn't be alive right now." Mary gazes at Paloma, now weeping in Isabel's arms.

Face-to-face, I realize she looks nothing like the old Mary, the person I trusted with every intimate detail of my life. Her face is sharp and cruel; her eyes glimmer with a mix of grief and hate. "How could you do this to me? After two years together, all day every day! I'm a daughter to you too," I insist. "And you're my—"

"Servant," she answers. It's a shock. I never thought of her that way. I thought she was one of the family—actually, the only family I had.

"Okay, ladies, enough," Marcos says, glancing at his watch. "It was a pleasure, but there's somewhere I have to be." He winks at me. "Take care of this," he says to Scars, and walks toward the graveyard.

"*Sí, señor.*" Scars smacks Mary across the face with an open palm, and she drops to the ground. Then he reaches for me.

On the ground below him, Mary grabs Scars's massive legs. "*No la toque a* Vivian," she warns Scars as he drags her across the ground. "Marcos—" Mary mimes the gesture of slitting Scars's throat.

Scars stops and shakes Mary off his leg. *If Mary said what I think she said, then Marcos is protecting me. But why?*

Then, by the cemetery gate, I see Paloma pointing at me, trying to get my attention. I look over and she tilts her head to the right, toward the long fence. "*Siga los cempasúchiles,*" Paloma says urgently.

Cempasúchiles? Where have I heard that word before? I suddenly remember Isabel in the cemetery, asking me to help her spread the marigold petals over Aurora's grave. I glance at Paloma, who is pointing toward the trail of orange petals that start at the cemetery gate and weave around the cemetery fence. *Siga los cempasúchiles. Follow the marigolds.*

Hoping I got the right message, I take off down the marigold path that winds around the cemetery fence, following the trail of orange petals. As I run, the petals crush beneath my shoes, releasing their sickly sweet scent into the air. To my surprise, I don't hear any footsteps behind me.

On the other side of the fence, people are leaving church and flooding back into the cemetery. In the light, their skeleton masks lose their power, becoming cheap Halloween decorations rather than the grim versions of death they were earlier. Some people are walking through the cemetery gates, little kids in their arms; others are cleaning the graves, pushing brooms back and forth, gathering trash from the night before in large black trash bags.

I finally glance back behind me. Scars is just standing at the top of the stairs, watching me. He's at least a foot taller than everyone around him, and it takes me a second to find Isabel, Mary, and Paloma huddled together at the cemetery gates. *Keep moving, Vivian. Siga los cempasúchiles.* I drop my head and focus on following the orange marigold path. It winds around the end of the fence, passes the farthest corner of the graveyard, and then leads to the door of the two-story white house. Hanging above the door is a gold-engraved picture of a coffin, with the words "Estella Funeraria" inside of it.

The path leads to a funeral home? What was Paloma trying to tell me?

The marigold path I'm following doesn't stop at the front door, but continues beneath the door, into the house.

Do it, Vivian. Turn the handle. Go in before anyone comes. I turn the doorknob, and the door opens into the Estella Funeraria.

I haven't been in a funeral home since Mom died. I remember how her casket was closed so we couldn't see her face, how Mary insisted that I wouldn't want to remember Mom that way. *But Mary did all of this to me. Did she help kill Mom, too?*

Gritting my teeth, I walk into the funeral parlor and close the door behind me. This somber, cold room couldn't be more different from the lively cemetery outside. The floor is covered with a deep red carpet, and there are two rows of black metal chairs, all facing a shiny silver coffin.

I creep forward along the thinning marigold path until it takes a sharp right turn at the coffin and disappears into an enclave, which is separated from the main room by a beaded curtain. I follow the flower petals through the curtain, the gold and black beads running in silky waves between my fingers. On the floor just inside the curtain, the path ends in a large orange cross of marigold petals. *But why did Paloma tell me to follow this path? Does this have anything to do with Mom?* When I look up, I see that I'm in a small chapel, glowing with candlelight. But it's unlike any chapel I've ever seen.

Taking up most of the altar is a life-sized skeleton wearing a white wedding dress. Her grinning skeleton face is partially covered by a long black wig, and a bridal veil, held on by a thin white crown, drapes down her back and over her lacy white dress. In her hands are a mean-looking golden sickle and the rolled-up weaving of Mom's face. *It's Santa Muerte: Just like the tattoo on Nick's back.*

Fear roots my feet to the ground when I suddenly realize I'm not alone. On the right side of the altar, almost hidden in the shadowy edge of the room, is a kneeling man. His head is tilted over his praying hands, and his shoulders shake gently as he murmurs rapidly in Spanish. Beside him, a ruby-topped cane leans against the edge of the altar.

I take a step backward, my heart thumping, and the wood creaks beneath my feet. Marcos snaps his head up. He grabs his cane, and wipes his cheeks with the back of his hand. "So you made it home," he says calmly. He wobbles to his feet and walks toward me, his ruby-topped cane knocking against the floor. "That's what the *cempasúchil* path is for, my dear. It helps the dead find their way home."

Don't let him see your fear. Don't give him that power. I suck in my breath as I watch his cane scatter the petals in the marigold cross. *He can't hurt me; I can always outrun him.* I try to look defiant and brave, but I can't stop my lips from trembling as he reaches out and gently turns my chin up to look at him. Marcos's pale gray eyes are almost translucent, and mirror my scared reflection back at me. "Santa Muerte," Marcos says, nodding toward the statue of the skeleton in the wedding dress. "She has been with me since I was very small, since my father passed. The Saint of Death, some call her," he adds, "but we call her Holy Death."

Okay, psycho.

Marcos drops his hand off my chin and gestures to the rolled-up weaving of Mom in the skeleton's hands. "A gift," he says. "Santa Muerte has been very good to me." Marcos draws a gold-tipped cigarette out of the front pocket of his suit, and lays it on the altar. Then he holds one out to me, and I shake my head. "One for her, one for me," he says, popping a cigarette between his lips and lighting it on a gold candle. "I had the perfect gift for her," he adds, "for your arrival, but I lost it. And such a beautiful pink diamond. I love roses, don't you?"

"What did you do to my mom?" I ask softly.

"Shhh . . ." Marcos says, running two cold fingers in a cross over my forehead.

He inhales deeply on his cigarette, and then exhales the smoke all over me, from head to toe. "We'll get to that later." Marcos takes another drag of his cigarette, and blows smoke over Santa Muerte.

"Desired Death of my heart," he chants, "we ask for your blessing." He blows smoke over me again, and through the smoke, I see Scars step into the room behind him. "Do not abandon Vivian from your protection," Marcos continues, gazing at the skeleton. "Guide her as you have guided me." He reaches into his coat pocket, pulls out a picture of me, and sets it on the altar. *He was praying over me? What the hell is going on?*

"Thank you for bringing her to me," he says to the skeleton, and then he turns, and his eyes lock on my face. There's a glossy sheen in his unwavering gaze, as if he's hypnotized.

I back up quickly, bumping into the altar. My picture falls off and floats to the floor. "Get away from me," I snarl.

"But she's been waiting for you a long time," Marcos says, gesturing to Santa Muerte. "And so have I."

"You can wait forever, you psycho!" I shriek. I turn around and shove the altar, and the skeleton of Santa Muerte tilts forward, tottering back and forth above us. Scars raises his gun in the air. Marcos tries to grab Scars's arm, but he isn't fast enough, and Scars slams the butt down on my head. There's an explosion in my temple, and the world goes black. Before I descend completely into darkness, I hear someone screaming.

Chapter Twenty-Six

My head hurts. Ouch.

Pain shoots like razors across my skull. The throbbing in my temples won't let me open my eyes, and the pain is making me feel fuzzy and unclear. I try to rub the lump on the back of my skull, but it hurts to touch.

When I finally open my eyes, I'm lying on a canopy bed in a dimly lit room, staring up at the mosquito netting hanging on all four sides of me. *Where am I? What happened?*

Then it all floods back in, trembling through my body and shaking me at my core: skeletons surrounding me, calling my name; trying to get past Marcos at the Santa Muerte altar; Scars hitting me on the head with the butt of his gun; tattooed hands forcing a pill down my throat, something that made me so sleepy I couldn't keep my eyes open.

My head swimming with fear, I sit up on the bed, push aside the mosquito netting, and stare out at the pale yellow room. It looks like a little girl's bedroom. The dresser has a miniature tea set and a dollhouse, and there are stuffed animals piled up under the window. *Whose room is this?* White-hot fear presses down on my heart. My body feels paralyzed for a moment, like in those nightmares where you know you're dreaming but you can't wake up.

I slowly put my bare feet on the floor and get up on shaky legs. Beneath my feet, the red carpet muffles the sound of my unsteady footsteps as I walk to the window. I pull back the curtain, and thick iron bars cut my view of the cemetery into stripes of dark night. *I'm still in the funeral home. I must have been asleep all day.* It still hurts to swallow from Scars's tattooed fingers pressing the pill down my throat. *What did Scars make me take?* There are only a few people left in the cemetery, gathered around a shiny marble tomb, playing a song on their guitars and singing in rough voices.

I have to get out of here.

I cross the room, silently pry the door open, and poke my head out into the long, red-carpeted hallway. It's lit by several small crystal chandeliers, hanging every few feet from the gilded ceiling. The hallway ends at the staircase, where Scars is standing watch, facing away from me. *Maybe I can get out of a window? They can't all be barred.*

Keeping my eyes locked on Scars's back, I tiptoe across the hall and quietly open the first door on the left. It's just a bathroom, with a huge marble tub, but no windows. I step back into the hallway and shut the bathroom door silently, grateful that the thick carpet muffles my footsteps.

Holding my breath, I tiptoe across the hallway to the last doorway. *Please let there be a window without bars.* Scars doesn't turn around as I open the door. *I'll just climb out and run down to the shore. From there, I can find someone to take me across the lake, to safety.*

I slip into the room and gently pull the door shut behind me. Even though it's dark in here, I can tell by the size of the room that I'm in the master bedroom. But there are only two windows in here: one is close to me, above a small altar striped with moonlight, and the other is on the far side of the room, near a bed covered with a mosquito net, like the one I woke up in.

Praying no one's sleeping in the bed, I tiptoe to the closest window and quietly pull the curtain aside a few inches. The moon glimmers off the thick black bars. *How am I going to get out of here?*

Under the window, there's a small table set up as an altar. The table is covered with a floor-length white sheet, and on the sheet is a large black-and-white photograph of a woman, several small sculptures of Santa Muerte, and a red velvet box, propped open in a patch of moonlight.

When I get closer, the smell of peroxide stings my nose. I look inside the box, and terror runs through me. In the box, there's a gleaming white skull. *But whose? Could it be Mom's? Is this what Paloma wanted me to find when she told me to follow the marigold path to the funeral home?*

I shove the thought out of my mind. *No! I won't believe it.* My hand touches something stiff on the altar, and I get another whiff of peroxide. As I pull my hand back, I see a filthy rag and a grimy bone with five smaller bones protruding from it. *Toes.* Dirt still clings to the edges.

Someone's been cleaning these bones. I shudder, but quickly bite my lip, resisting the urge to scream. *Breathe*, I tell myself, and force a breath in and out.

What now? I look across the room toward the other window. I don't want to go anywhere near the veiled bed, but the only other way out is through Scars. *I have to try.*

I move forward slowly. My chest has a solid rock in it, trying to pull me backward. *What if someone jumps out and attacks me? What do I do?* I try to recall the judo moves I learned for *Zombie Killer:* Two fingers in the eyes. Flat hand across the nose, and up, so it goes through the brain. *Please don't let me have to use them.*

I finally make it to the window, staying several feet away from the bed. But when I flick open the curtains, the same bars close me off from the outside world. *I only have one choice now: to try to make it past Scars.*

I let the curtains fall shut, and turn to tiptoe out of the room, but I can't stop myself from glancing at the bed. *What if Marcos is in it, asleep, or waiting for me to come close enough to grab my ankle and pull me under the bed?* I squint through the mosquito netting, and shapes start forming out of the darkness: the curve of a skinny knee under a sheet, an arm hanging off a mattress.

Staying an arm's length away, I step carefully up to the canopied bed and pull the mosquito netting back slightly.

It's Mom.

Chapter Twenty-Seven

UNTIL NOW, WHEN I IMAGINED my mom dead, she looked just like she did when she was alive, except maybe with a little more makeup. Since Mom never left the house without looking her best, I thought she would look that way in death too. I imagined cherry-red lipstick painting her lips into a smile, smoky eye shadow bringing out the pink tones in her skin, her cheeks powdered to a rosy peach color. Of course, I tried not to think about it. But some images keep coming back to haunt you.

Like this one.

Mom's face is ashen and bloodless; her Adam's apple gouges out of her skeletal neck. Her wan lips droop into a creased frown, and her eyelids are crossed with tiny blue veins. A flowered bobby pin clips her hair back, so that her heart-shaped mole stands out against her pale white face. Diamonds circle her neck, her wrists. Every finger has a diamond ring, and from her ears hang giant drops of emeralds. She is still beautiful. But she is not my mom anymore: she is completely *lifeless*.

Time slows to a standstill, and it's just me, alone in this room. I only feel something squeezing out of my eyes, wet and tingly, and streaming into my mouth. My head begins pounding the same unsteady beat as my chest, and my ears ring like a bomb just went off. *Mom's dead.* My knees buckle, and I crumple to the floor.

I am aware of only a few things:

My dress is bunched around my waist.

The red carpet is itchy on my thighs.

My mom is dead.

With my cheek against the dense carpet, I gaze out at the endless expanse of red, not really seeing anything. *Maybe the earth will open up and swallow me. I can hope for that.*

I have no idea how long I've been on the floor, waiting for the earth to swallow me whole, when I hear Isabel's words in my head: *Someday the pain ends and you stop being so afraid.* I push my palms against the red carpet, forcing myself to sit up, and then pull my dress down over my legs. *You only fear what you think you can't handle.*

Maybe I can handle this.

I have no idea if I can, but some of the strength Mom told me about is pulsing through my veins, and I'm starting to believe her: *I'm stronger than I think.* I made it all the way across Mexico, survived Nick's betrayal, and got away from Scars (twice). *I can handle this.* I crawl onto my knees, and then waver to my feet, gripping the bed frame so hard my knuckles are turning white. *I have to survive this. For Mom.*

When I'm standing over her, the mosquito net dark and forbidding between us, with sorrow filling every inch of me, I hear something, or at least I think I do: a gasp, or a sigh, or maybe a creak in the floor? I can't tell. I stare at her gaunt face, searching for any sign of life, but I can't see any. *If she's dead, I will survive, I will move on with my life, somehow.* I hear the noise again, a faint shudder, like wind seeping under a door. *But what if that wasn't the wind? What if she sighed, or gasped, or . . .*

I slowly reach toward Mom, pushing past the dark netting, and let my finger hover over her wrist. Tears dribble off my nose and dissolve in her blond curls. *Just find out.* I reach farther, until I feel her cool skin with my fingertip, but I'm afraid to get closer, to break the moment like an egg and see all its yellow insides drain out. After what feels like hours, I rest my index finger on her exposed wrist.

And feel a pulse.

The clammy air slides down my throat and unties the knot in my chest. *She's alive!* "Mom!" I push the mosquito netting aside and crawl onto her bed, wrapping my arms around her and pressing my head to her chest. She doesn't move, but I can feel the steady beating of her heart. "Mom?" I put my hands on her shoulders and shake her lightly, but there's no response. "Please wake up, Mom."

"She can't hear you, I'm afraid." Marcos's smell rushes ahead of him, a mix of cologne and cigarette smoke.

My blood stops pumping; my entire body stills so completely I can feel each beat of my heart. It feels like someone pressed the brake, and I've shuddered to a stop.

In the doorway, Marcos's eyes are pale silver, and he is gazing at me with the same obsessed look he had in the chapel. He's still wearing his red silk suit, and he leans heavily on his cane.

"I'm sorry about that," Marcos says as he walks across the room, dragging one leg behind him. Scars follows him like a feral dog, ducking his head to get through the doorway. "Scars has anger issues," Marcos says calmly. "But he has learned his lesson." When Scars raises his head, he has two long knife cuts down his face. "He cannot be allowed to act like an animal, wouldn't you agree?" Marcos asks. As he moves closer to me, the pressure in the air thickens, building an invisible wall between us, and the tension almost flattens me against the bed.

I jump off the bed, and each word bleeds out of my mouth, filled with confusion and rage. "What did you do to my mom?"

Marcos studies me carefully, as if he's honestly considering the question. "We are very close," he says, "your mom and I. If she were awake, she'd tell you so herself." From a few feet away, Marcos's albino alligator shoes, so rare even Dad can't afford them, glimmer against the red carpet. "But someone may have given her a little too much." He glowers at Scars, his anger burning across the room. Marcos steps up to the edge of the bed, places his finger on Mom's eyelid, and gently lifts upward. It's white underneath. "Just sleeping pills. She should wake in a few hours."

I know all about sleeping pills. Pierre takes them to get a few hours of sleep before his shoots so that he won't have bags under his eyes. Mom always refused to let me take them. She said that they weren't anything to mess with; an overdose of sleeping pills could kill you. "What do you want from us?" I ask, flinching as the question pops out of my mouth.

"The question isn't what I want from you," Marcos says, "it's what you want from me." He leans down and strokes Mom's cheek with the back of his hand. "I just want to love you, and I hope that you will do me the favor of loving me back." He twirls one of Mom's curls with his fingers, tilting his head at me curiously. "What do you want?"

"I want to go home."

"So did your mom," he says fondly. "She wanted so much to be freed, to be back with you and your . . ." He scowls as he says the word "*father*." He shakes his head. "Your mother hasn't learned to love me yet, I'm afraid, but she will. She just can't see what's good for her, stubborn woman," he says. "She's fought to go home like a *toro*, a bull. But then again, she had you to go home to. What do you have to return to?"

What do I have? That's a good question. I used to have everything a girl could want: famous parents, a superstar boyfriend, a best friend, and a loyal bodyguard. But once everyone thought Mom was dead, I lost it all: Dad tried to kill himself, Pierre cheated on me with Sparrow, Mary sent me down here to die. *But I still have Mom—if I can get her out of here alive.*

"I have money," I say, my voice trembling, "and if you let us go, I'll pay anything you want."

"This isn't about money," Marcos says, one lip lifting up into an insulted grimace. "The more you have, the less it matters, I've found," he says, inspecting the ruby on top of his cane. "What kind of man do you think I am?"

A crazy one who kidnaps movie stars and keeps a drugged woman in his bedroom? I scoot farther around the bed, keeping the mattress between us. "Why were you at Isabel's?" I ask.

"Looking for you," he says, stepping closer to me. "When you and Nicolas didn't show up, I sent Scars to find you. And when Scars's car . . ."

Marcos turns his hand upside down, and I remember flipping over and over, glass shattering around me.

". . . I went looking for you myself."

"Stay away from me." I shuffle behind the bed's headboard, gripping the bedpost like a shield.

"But I'm not going to hurt you," he whispers, and I can't tell if he's talking to Mom or me. Then he leans down and rearranges the flowered bobby pin in Mom's hair, clipping her bangs back from her face. "There," he says. "Much better." He hovers so closely their lips are almost touching, and then he moves his lips away from hers, and kisses her heart-shaped mole. "Still so beautiful," he says, leering at Scars. "Even like this."

Scars scuffles toward Marcos nervously, his shoulders hunched and head down. *"Lo siento, señor."*

Marcos glares at Scars, and then he kneels down beside Mom and runs his hands through her hair, a look of crazed adoration on his face. "Pearl always liked to look her best," he says. "She used to say, 'Don't ever let me leave the house without my best face on!'"

I grew up hearing the same thing. How did he know that?

"Get away from her!" I snap, and before the last word is out of my mouth, Scars leaps to his feet and grabs both of my arms in one giant hand. I try not to cringe from the pain in my wrists.

"*No es necesario*," Marcos says to Scars, glancing up from Mom's lifeless face and staring directly at me. "Vivian isn't going anywhere." Marcos gazes back down at Mom, but Scars doesn't let go; he just squeezes tighter and tighter, until my wrists start to pulse with pain.

"Ow," I whimper.

Marcos glances up, and then he's on his feet, grabbing Scars around the neck and squeezing. The gashes across Scars's face turn scarlet and bulge out, his snake tattoos squirm and writhe under the pressure, and his breath becomes raspy and urgent. "*¡Idiota!*" Marcos snarls at him. "*¡No toque!*" With his arm extended, Marcos lowers Scars to his knees. "Never touch her again! *¿Comprende?*" He lets go, and Scars falls forward, crumpling to the ground by Marcos's feet.

As Scars lies on the floor, gasping for breath, I retreat behind the headboard, rubbing the skin around my aching wrists. "Did that guy work for you too?" I ask, my voice shaking as I point to the red velvet box on the altar. Between the black-and-white picture and the small sculptures of Santa Muerte, the skull glistens in its red velvet grave.

Marcos walks across the room and pushes aside the white sheet draping off the altar. On the floor beneath the altar, there are two wooden crates full of bones, laid out perfectly side by side. "That's *mi madre*," he says sadly. "Your mother, she's been cleaning them, preparing Mama for her eternal rest."

"Why?"

"Because they dug up *mi madre*, and she needs cleaning before returning to Santa Muerte," Marcos says. "And because your mother wants to please me, of course, after everything I've done for her."

"What do you mean? I don't understand," I say to Marcos. "Why are you doing this? You don't even know her."

"Don't know her?" Marcos says, returning to Mom's bedside. "Don't know her? I loved her!"

"You didn't love her," I say, suddenly seeing Marcos clearly for who he is: a rich, crazy stalker who fell in love with Mom on TV, like a million other men have, and thought he couldn't live without her. It's not unheard of. A man stalked Sparrow's cousin for months, claiming he loved her, and locked her up in his cellar until the police broke her out. *But somehow, I don't think the police are coming this time.* I look down at Mom's limp body. "You may have seen her movies, but you don't know who she really is."

"I don't know the woman who betrayed me, who ruined my life?" Marcos slams his fist against the wall near my head, and his hand makes a loud cracking sound as it crashes through the wall. He yanks his fist out of the hole, drywall crumbling with it, and his hand's bleeding like crazy, but he doesn't seem to notice that he's dripping blood all over the bed. It's like Marcos has split in half: his calm, in-control side disappears, and a hysterical madman takes his place. "The woman who let me rot in prison for fifteen years," he yells, "while she married that man you call your father?"

What is he talking about?

"I don't know the woman who took everything from me?" Marcos continues, his voice now an unrestrained roar. "Who took my freedom? My life?" He shakes the headboard so hard it rattles against the floor, and drops of his blood fling around the room. "I don't know the woman who stole our daughter?"

Chapter Twenty-Eight

OUR DAUGHTER?

The room spins around me, and I suddenly can't get my feet steady beneath me. I stagger backward as my body breaks out in a hot sweat. *I don't believe him. It can't be true.* It's like someone took my world and spun it around, and I'm just barely holding on. *My mom couldn't have been with him. He lives in the mountains in Mexico, and she's a big Hollywood star.*

"You're lying!" I throw my hands up to shove his lies away from me, and my foot catches on the bed frame. I stumble to the ground, landing painfully on my tailbone.

Looming above me, Marcos draws his eyebrows close together under the tense V on his forehead. I can hear his breath cut angrily through the air between us as he looks down at me. And then, a calm expression settles back over his face, and his mouth contorts into a smile.

My smile.

A tremor rocks me from head to foot, because that's when I see it, and every bit of me wishes I hadn't: the same face I see in the mirror every day. The strong Roman nose that I thought I'd inherited from my deceased grandparents, the square cheekbones, too sharp for a girl's face, the lips that puff out in the eternal pout my mom has envied for years. *Just like your dad's,* I remember Mom muttering as she locked my bedroom windows.

My mouth drops open at the shocking resemblance, and I wonder how I didn't see it before. *I wasn't looking for it.* I'm trying to take this all in, but my mind keeps getting caught on one horrible thought: *If I'm his daughter, am I a monster too?*

Marcos leans down and holds his hand out to pull me up, but I don't take it. I climb to my feet, holding on to the bedpost to steady myself.

"I didn't know about you until you were fourteen years old," Marcos says, shaking his head. "All those years in prison, watching your mom on TV, with that man you call your father, and never knowing that his daughter was actually yours? Can you imagine how lonely I was when I found out?" Marcos asks, his voice distraught. "But when you were nominated for the Oscar—well deserved, by the way," he adds, "the news showed a special about you, and I did the math." He taps his temple twice with his index finger. "Your mom and I were in a relationship when she got pregnant with you," he says. "She hadn't even met that director yet."

I look down at Mom's still body on the bed, watching how the diamonds around her throat rise slightly up and down with each shallow breath. *Can it be true? Why would Mom have lied to me all this time? But why else would she be here, with a man who looks more like me than my father ever did?*

Marcos awkwardly puts his unhurt hand on my shoulder. I want to pull away, but I don't: I just freeze in place under his heavy touch. "I'm sorry I was never there for you as a child. I know how hard it is to grow up without a father. I had to do the same," he says. "But I promise you'll never have to be without me again." Marcos wipes his bloody fist on his pants, and the blood just fades into the red silk. *I wonder how much blood those pants have soaked up.* "I would've come for you sooner," Marcos continues, his uninjured hand still resting uncomfortably on my shoulder, "but when I found out that you were *my* daughter, not *his*, I still had two more years behind bars."

"I don't believe you," I say, studying how he nervously chews on his lower lip, and how he half smiles, with just one side of his mouth lifting and the other frowning. *Just like I do.* I shrug his hand off my shoulder. "Why would

Mom be with a man like you?"

"I can be very persuasive when I want to be," Marcos says. "Your mom was almost as young as you are now, new to the movie business, and she would have done anything to become an actress. And I was young, and rich, and connected, and absolutely loved her. We could have been great together, our little family. But at least we'll get to be a family now," he adds. "How do you think she got her first role? Sheer talent?"

Mom's first role was as Medusa, in an Oscar-winning film Dad directed. She fell in love and married him in the first three months of shooting. *But was she dating someone else at the time?*

It's like I'm looking at myself through a kaleidoscope. The girl I thought I was is breaking into bits and floating away, mixing with this person I don't know, this daughter of a murderer. I suddenly remember a script I read for a movie Mom wouldn't let me act in. It was about the "killer gene," the gene that supposedly runs in families, causing several people in one family to become serial killers. *Did Mom not want me to somehow activate the "killer" button?*

"When I got out of prison and took her back," Marcos continues, "I thought I could trust her. But even today she betrayed me," he says, an angry red flush starting to creep up his cheeks. "She begged me to let her go to the play, and I thought it was because she wanted to be with *me*. But when Scars brought her to the church, she screamed for help. Can you believe that? After all I've done for her?"

So that's how I heard Mom's voice in the church.

"Scars had to bring her back here, but she should have been here anyway, cleaning *mi madre* up," he continues. "If your mom hadn't screamed when she saw you, she would be done by now." Marcos shakes his head, glancing at the dirty foot bone on the altar. "But now you get to help."

"I will never help you," I say between gritted teeth.

"If you'd met your grandmother," Marcos says, "you'd feel differently." He picks up the foot bone from the altar, and a clump of mud comes off in his hand. "I guess it's not too late." He gets a Q-tip out of the wooden crate and starts cleaning the toes very gently, using the Q-tip to get in all of the little crevices. "You're a lot like her, you know." Marcos holds the half-clean foot out to me, but I clasp my hands behind my back and shake my head furiously.

"Never."

"You know, you can go anytime," Marcos says. "I'm not keeping you here. The door's unlocked."

"I'm not leaving without my mom."

"Then I can't help you." Marcos shrugs and lays the foot on the altar, beside the red box. "But if we don't clean *mi madre* and get her back in the ground, she won't have anywhere to come home to," he says sadly. He carefully lifts the skull out of the box and sets it on the table, and then he takes off his red silk jacket and gently layers the inside of the box with it. "Do you want your grandmother's lost soul wandering the streets?"

I glare at him. "She's not my grandmother."

"Denial doesn't fit you," Marcos says calmly, picking up the foot bone and rubbing the last of the dirt off with his red handkerchief. "When your grandmother's soul returns for the Day of the Dead and sees her bones dressed in new clothes"—he nods toward his red silk jacket lining the box—"she'll see that she wasn't forgotten, and she can rest more peacefully."

"She'll never rest peacefully with you for a son!" I snap.

My skull vibrates under the force of his hand, and my cheek stings with fierce pain before I even realize he's slapped me. I clap my hand to my cheek, my skin burning under my palm.

"The bones have to be in the right order," Marcos says, his voice pleasant again. He places his mother's foot bone in the red box. "How can she stand up to meet Santa Muerte if she doesn't have her feet under her?"

Cupping my cheek with one hand, I glance up at his calm face. *It's like he doesn't realize he hit me.* The hairs on my arms and legs stand straight up, and the back of my neck prickles with terror.

Marcos lifts one of the wooden crates of shiny white bones from underneath the altar. "The stories these bones could tell," he says, taking a bone out of the crate and placing it into the red box. "*Mi madre* always wanted a girl, but all she had was me," he continues, "and I was a constant disappointment." He places the rest of the bones carefully in the red velvet box, and then reaches for the second crate. "And when I wanted to move to America to be with your mother, *mi madre* refused to allow it. Nobody disobeyed *mi madre*'s orders. But I was young, and I left anyway. The day I walked out the door, she disowned me for betraying her."

I glance over at Mom. She's still deathly pale, but I can see her chest rise with each breath. *Did she know all of this? And why didn't she tell me?*

Marcos continues stacking the bones from the second crate into the red velvet box, crossing them like an elaborate puzzle, one on top of the other. "When I moved to California, *mi madre* cut tears under her eyes," he continues. He draws two long, curved lines beneath his eyes. "Here, and here. So she'd always remember how much I had hurt her." He shakes his head, and then reaches into the second wooden crate, fishes out the last bones, and places them carefully on top of the pile. "Scars learned that from her."

I glance at the black-and-white picture of the woman on the altar and try to imagine her with two knife lines cut down her face. *Why would she cut her face? Just to punish her son? And what would that do to him?*

"When I asked your mother to marry me," he continues, "she said no, and then she left me for that director." Marcos's eyes well up with tears. "*Mi madre* refused to see me. I had nobody," he says, picking up the skull from the altar. "I gave up *everything* for Pearl."

Tears drip down his cheeks, and my heart lurches unexpectedly. *So I feel a little sorry for him. I can't help it.*

"I was arrested a month later, and I never saw *mi madre* again. She died while I was in prison." Marcos grips the skull so tightly his knuckles turn white. "She died cursing my name, saying that when I abandoned her for an American woman, I betrayed my family," he says. "I would never betray my family!" Marcos places the skull carefully on top of the bone pile, now almost two feet tall from head to feet. "I would still give up everything for your mother," he says. "And for you. You're all I have," he adds.

Standing there, watching him leaning on his cane, I feel his sadness. He gave up his whole life for my mother, and she ditched him, and took his child with her. *Maybe he's not all bad.*

"So I built a mausoleum, a place where we can all be together, forever," he continues. He closes the red box, and looks at me. "Family always comes first with me, *mi hija*, unlike that director, whose work always came before you."

"Maybe so," I say, staring at the closed red box on the altar. "But at least my dad didn't lock my mom in some room like a prisoner—"

Marcos grabs my chin and squeezes, so I am forced to look at him. "I'm doing this for you," he says. "*I* am your father. Me! Not him!" He pushes me backward by my chin until I'm jammed against the altar. "Do you hear me?"

I swear I can feel my jaw cracking. *I was wrong—he's all bad.* "Let go," I plead, pain shooting through my skull. "Please."

Marcos drops his hand from my chin and backs up. He stares at his hands like he's shocked at what he's done. "You'll learn to be part of this family," he says in a softer voice. "You'll learn to love me."

"I'll never love you!" I scream.

Marcos snaps his fingers and points toward Mom's bed, and Scars wrenches my arm behind me. He marches me over to Mom's headboard and holds my arm down while he handcuffs me to the bed frame.

"My little girl," Marcos says, his stinking cigarette breath hot on my face. "How gutsy you are. How full of life, like your grandmother." He smiles. "After I lay her to rest," Marcos says, nodding to the box of bones, "we'll go somewhere, just the three of us. Somewhere no one will ever find you."

With Scars behind him, Marcos grabs the box and marches out of the room, leaving me handcuffed to the bed of my beautiful, unconscious Mom.

* * *

With my hand locked to the bed, the walls close around me, and the lingering smell of Marcos's cologne is suffocating, tightening my throat until I can't breathe. *What do I do now?* Mom lies placid and still below me, her rising and falling chest the only sign that she's alive.

"Mom?" I whisper, but there's no answer.

I'm standing handcuffed to the bedpost, wishing Mom would wake up and help me figure out how to get out of here, when I see the flowered bobby pin poking out of her hair. A line pops into my head, one I repeated dozens of times to get the right balance of hope and desperation that the Zombie Killer is known for. *All that stands between me and the end of the world . . . is a bobby pin.*

Of course. The improbable genius of the plan hits me, and I lean over Mom, straining my arm to reach the bobby pin clipped in her hair.

We must have shot that scene two dozen times to make it authentic.

Uncuffing yourself from a mutilated zombie is no easy task. I run my tongue over the tooth I chipped from forcing the bobby pin into the lock with my teeth. After twenty tries, Dad had to bend the bobby pin into a U shape for me to believably pry the handcuffs open. *But does that work outside the studio? Dad insists on authenticity in his films—but is it authentic enough?*

I close my eyes, trying to remember Dad's instructions.

First, take off the plastic cover. I steady the bobby pin in my free hand, poking the plastic end between my thumb and forefinger. Then I clamp my teeth around the plastic and slowly draw it off the bobby pin. *First step. Check. But what makes me think I can do it this time when Dad had to do it for me last time?*

I make sure that I have the pin securely between my fingers, and then I insert the bobby pin in the lock, push my handcuffed hand toward the bed, and pull up on the bobby pin. The metal is hard against my wrist bone, reminding me that I'm basing my whole escape plan on a movie scene that wasn't real in the first place. But I feel the bobby pin bending, slowly, beneath my fingers. *Don't crack. Please don't crack.*

I wiggle out the now L-shaped pin, insert it the other way in the lock, and try to bend the metal as slowly as humanly possible. I have to bend it into a U shape without it breaking. *That's the only way it works—in the movies, anyway.*

After five excruciating minutes and the blood nearly completely drained out of my arm, I feel two right angles. *A perfect U.*

Please work. Please work. Please work.

I mumble these words under my breath, until I can't hear them anymore, and then I turn the pin.

SNAP! The bobby pin breaks in the lock, taking with it my last chance of escape—and Mom's last chance at life.

* * *

The broken end of the bobby pin falls out of the lock and bounces against the bed frame with a *plink*. It's the loudest sound I've ever heard—louder than gunshots and steel crushing, than shattering glass and crowds chanting my name. *It's all over. Marcos will take us somewhere where no one will ever find us.*

"Let us out!" I yell, banging my handcuffed hand against the bed. "We want out!" Tears roll down my face, gathering in the corners of my lips and dripping from my chin. I pound on the handcuff with my other fist until pain pulses across my knuckles, and then I start to scream: soul-wrenching, heart-ripping screams.

When my voice is hoarse and my throat feels raw from screaming, I hear footsteps outside the room. *Marcos is coming.* I pull against my handcuffs, the metal shredding my skin. *There has to be a way out.* As the footsteps get closer, I bang my wrist against the metal as hard as I can, hoping to break the cuff. *No luck.*

Find a weapon. I scan the bed for something to protect myself with, something within arm's reach. On the end of each bedpost is an antique brass ornament, shaped like a blunt letter opener with curlicues on each side. *Better than nothing.* With one hand cuffed to the headboard, I twist the nearest brass ornament until it comes off. It slips out of my grip and bounces under the bed. *Damnit!* I stretch my leg out and try to kick it toward me, but my foot just misses.

The footsteps stop just outside the room. Someone pokes his face in, just long enough for me to look him in the eyes, with no Don Juan mask to cover his cruel face:

Nick.

Chapter Twenty-Nine

IN THE DIMLY LIT BEDROOM, Nick's red jersey shines like a fat drop of blood. *If it isn't the last person in the world I want to see.*

"What are you doing here?" I growl, yanking repeatedly on the handcuff until the skin around my wrist feels rubbed raw.

"I can explain," Nick says, edging into the room. "But we've got to hurry. We don't have long until—"

"Until you kill me?"

"Until Marcos notices these are missing." Nick takes a key ring out of his pocket, and the keys jingle together, frighteningly loud in the pressed silence of the bedroom.

I remember the cart of ceramic skeletons in the plaza, the way their bones tinkled together in air thick with kerosene. "I'm not trying to scare you—"

"You don't scare me, you son of a bitch!" I lunge at him, but my wrist bone slams against the inside of the handcuff, shooting pain up and down my arm. "Everything you said about being glad I was there, accidentally meeting me on the bus, helping me get to Rosales—that was a big cover-up, wasn't it? For your godfather?"

Nick steps farther into the room, staying carefully out of arm's reach. "Yes, but I didn't know he was going to hurt you, I swear to God. Marcos just asked me to follow an American girl to make sure she got safely to Rosales."

"Don't bother lying to me. You knew exactly who I was the whole time!" I prod around with my foot until I feel the brass ornament stab the sole of my shoe. "And all those hours we talked about my life, all those things I shared with you . . ." My voice cracks. "You were probably laughing inside."

"I wasn't. I swear I wasn't. I'll prove it to you. But right now—we've gotta get you out of here." He grabs my handcuffed wrist and tries to force the key into the lock. "Hold still!" he says. I'm pressed against the bed frame, adrenaline shooting through my body, and I'm confused about whether I want to kiss him or kill him.

"Get your hands off me!" I lean down, the movement

tweaking my handcuffed wrist so it pulses with pain. Ignoring my throbbing wrist, I grab the brass ornament with my free hand and swing it at him. He jumps back, a brass curlicue narrowly missing his pretty face. "Why should I believe anything you say?"

"Because Marcos will be here in less than an hour, and we have to be gone by then." He shakes the keys in front of me. "And I have the keys to your handcuffs. If you'll let me unlock you, we can get to the boat before Marcos gets here."

"Whose boat?" I ask, shifting the weapon to my handcuffed hand so I can rub the searing pain out of my wrist.

"My cousin Antonio's meeting us in the cove in an hour. He'll take us to the American consulate in Rosales, but he can only wait for ten minutes, and then he'll leave without us."

"Why a measly boat?" I say sarcastically. "If you're making it up, why not go big? How about a private jet, or a rescue helicopter?"

"What can I do to make you believe me?" Nick asks. "I'm trying to save your life! And I can get you out of here, if you'll just let me unlock you—"

"You really think I'd let you anywhere near me?"

"Here, unlock your own handcuffs." He tosses the keys to me and I catch them with my free hand, making sure to hold on to my makeshift weapon in my other hand. *What do I have to lose? I can either wait here for Marcos, or try to trust Nick a little. If the key doesn't work, then he's betrayed me again. But what if he's really trying to help me?* I insert the small key into the lock. *But why would Nick help me now?* I turn the key and the cuffs unlock with a quiet click.

"Is this a trick?" I ask. *Otherwise, why is he helping me? Won't Marcos kill Nick for betraying him?*

"No trick," Nick says. "I didn't know what Marcos wanted. He used me to get to you, but I'm not going to let him hurt you." He lifts Mom up in his arms, her neck bent backward so her mouth's hanging open. "Follow me."

Gripping my weapon, I follow Nick as he moves swiftly across the room, toward the table under the window, where Marcos kept his mother's bones. *My grandmother.* My stomach wrenches.

"Do you believe me yet?" Nick asks, stopping beside the dressing table.

"Maybe," I admit, loosening my grip a little on my makeshift weapon. *Why else would he unlock my handcuffs? Doesn't he have everything to lose too?* "But I wouldn't be here if I hadn't lost my bag on that bus. Or was that your fault, too?"

"I had nothing to do with the bus breaking down," Nick says. "But I kind of—had something to do with your missing bag. I didn't want to do it, but Marcos made me promise to dispose of it. I didn't have a choice. It would have been too easy for you to slip away if you had money and a passport," he explains. "Besides, I knew I'd be there to protect you."

Nick stole my bag? He took the only things I owned, and lied about it to my face? I'm so angry now hot tears are filling my eyes. I tighten my grip on the brass ornament again, still small and sharp in my hands. "Protect me from who?" I ask. "You? You're just like the rest of them. You're no better than Scars."

Nick flinches like I just smacked him across the face. "But I can be, Vivian." He presses his knee against the side of the altar, and it moves a few feet to the left. Beneath it is an opening in the floor, with stairs disappearing into the darkness.

"Just give me a chance," Nick says, stepping onto the top stair. "Stay close," he whispers. He climbs quietly down two flights of stairs, and I follow him closely, not wanting to be more than a foot away from Mom. "Marcos had a tunnel dug to transport his goods," Nick says, stepping off the last stair into the dank, smelly basement. He crosses the basement quickly and stops in front of a dark, gaping hole in the wall. "It runs from here to the lake, so it's really steep and floods when it rains, but I can get you out this way."

I peek around Nick into the narrow, concrete tunnel. *But how do I know he's not still working for Marcos? Getting rid of the evidence?* I test both edges of the brass ornament, turning it over so the sharpest side is facing Nick. "Give me one reason I should believe you."

"Because I'm going to get you out of here," Nick says.

He did unlock my handcuffs and show me the way to the tunnel. Maybe Nick isn't lying—maybe he's going to help us.

"There's a rowboat at the end of the tunnel," Nick continues. "All we have to do is follow the shoreline left until we see Antonio's boat. It has a Santa Muerte flag on it. Remember Santa Muerte?"

I nod, remembering the creepy skeleton in the wedding dress tattooed onto Nick's back, and the way he trembled when I traced my fingers across his skin.

"We'll follow the tunnel all the way down to the lake," Nick adds, ducking into the narrow opening. "If anything happens to me, keep going. Don't look back."

If Nick were still working for Marcos, would he think something could "happen" to him? I let my hand relax around the ornament. *If he's warning me about it, couldn't that mean he's running for his life too?*

From above us, there's the tapping of two feet, and then four, as they walk across the funeral parlor. *They're coming.* Hoping I'm making the right choice, I quickly follow Nick into the tunnel.

The tunnel's a tube of concrete, just tall enough for me to stand up in. Water seeps through the cracks in the concrete above my head, flooding the tunnel with cold, murky water up to my ankles. Bare lightbulbs hang from the ceiling, flickering a sickly yellow hue, so it's not dark exactly, but that kind of eerie twilight where ghosts should materialize out of thin air.

Water sloshes against the concrete as I follow Nick down the tunnel, the brass ornament tucked uncertainly in my hand. "Why are you helping us?" I ask.

Nick readjusts Mom in his arms so her blond hair doesn't drag in the water. "Remember that boy we met? The one that followed you in the forest and drew my gun in the dirt?"

I nod, watching how our shadows launch themselves at the concrete walls.

"That boy didn't call you the White Devil. He called me a criminal, and he was right," Nick says. "And that's all I thought I was until I met you. Then I thought . . . maybe if I was with you, I could be something different."

"Different?"

"Better," Nick says.

"You can be."

"If you were really Ines, an ordinary girl, maybe. But you're the most famous girl in the world, and the only thing my godfather wants."

In the rising water of the tunnel, my feet slide out from under me, and I press my palms against both walls to keep standing. The sharp end of the brass ornament stabs my right hand, and I realize I've forgotten about my makeshift weapon. *Maybe because I believe Nick's trying to help us. Or maybe because I care about him, and I think he cares about me too.* "But you're not ordinary either," I say, carefully holding myself up in the frigid water. "You can act, and make fires, and kiss like a genius."

Nick smiles, briefly lighting up the dingy tunnel, and I could kiss the dimples in his tan cheeks. "I have to get you out of here," he says, his smile fading. "I've lost everyone else I loved. I won't lose you."

He loves me! The brass ornament slips out of my hand and splashes as it lands in the water. *Nick loves me!* "I love—"

"I know," Nick says.

A boom echoes through the tunnel, and voices race toward us, garbled and incomprehensible. Every sound rattles through my brain: the roar of their voices, water sloshing against the walls, the pounding of their feet.

"Vivian!" Marcos yells. His voice echoes around me, chasing me down the concrete tube. I try to run, but I'm almost up to my knees in water, so I trudge ahead as fast as I can, my feet sliding across the slippery concrete.

"Hurry!" I wedge my hands against the walls and focus on placing each foot carefully on the concrete, one after the other. *Just don't fall.*

The ceiling of the tunnel gets abruptly lower, and we have to crouch to keep forging ahead. "We're almost there," Nick says. "Hear that?"

I hear the sound of waves echoing down the tunnel. *The lake.*

We're here.

Outside the tunnel, rain is streaking across the small circle of sky. Slices of razor-sharp rain bounce off the water, each drop a wrinkle in the lake's dark flesh. The roar of rain on the top of the concrete tunnel pounds in my ears.

"Vivian!" Marcos's voice rolls down the tunnel, the pressure of it pushing me forward. "Come back here!"

The cold concrete bites my fingers as I wrap my hand around the lip of the tunnel and scoot out of the narrow opening onto the moonlit beach, my feet immediately sinking into the sand. My legs burn from crouching in the entrance, and the rain is pounding wet needles into my skinned kneecaps. Nick is standing in the sand beside me, Mom cradled tightly in his arms.

We're on a tiny beach, a dark, twenty-foot crescent of pebbles and sand. To my right is an old rickety dock, and tied to it is the small wooden boat Nick picked me up in.

Nick carries Mom across the tiny beach to the boat. "Get in," he says. He lays her down gently on the wet floor, and I swing my leg over the side, instantly feeling the sting of the freezing rain pelt my thighs. The boat rocks under my weight, and water slaps against the side, showering Mom and me with icy water.

Coughing racks Mom's brittle body, and a groan sputters out of her mouth. The muscles twitch below her eyelids, and then she wrenches her eyes open, her pupils huge black circles, the whites of her eyes shot up with red veins. They roll upward as she tries to focus on me. She blinks rapidly in the rain, her breath tearing out of her chest.

"Mom?" *She's awake. Thank God.* I curve my hands around her cheeks and try to hold her face steady. "Mom, it's me."

Mom's head rocks back and forth, each gaunt cheek deathly white against the dark wood floor. She opens her trembling mouth, and her lips form a word that never comes.

"It's me, Vivian," I repeat.

Mom groans, and somewhere in there I hear the vowels of my name: "Viiiiiviiiiiaaaaann?"

"I'm here." Her skin is thin as paper in my cupped hands. "We're leaving." I glance over at Nick, who's untying the boat from the rickety dock. His fingers are shaking in the pelting rain, and the rope keeps falling out of his hands.

Mom's fingers desperately grasp the air, and I place my hand over hers. "Get . . . out . . ." she moans.

"We're already out," I whisper, and her eyes drop closed, rapidly twitching under the lids.

Nick drops the end of the rope into the boat and hands me the oars. "Hold on to these," he says, wading out into the ankle-deep water. "The lake's pretty shallow here, so I'll push us out," he says. As Nick pushes us across the shallow lake, the bottom of the boat scraping the sandy floor, I glance across the dark, stormy water, toward Rosales. *We're going to make it to safety. Nick will come back to L.A. with me, and we'll start over, Mom and Dad, me, and the boy I love.*

Chapter Thirty

IT ALL HAPPENS SO FAST.

It reminds me of the car accident with Scars, before the car's first flip, when the world sped up and shattered to glass around me. Now, echoing out of the tunnel, Scars's guttural howl breaks the sky like crushing steel, and the sound of his angry voice rains down around me in dark slivers.

In the moonlight, I see Marcos emerge from the tunnel into the whipping rain, a scowl on his face as deeply creased as his soaking red suit. He stands unsteadily on the tiny, dark beach, holding on to the lip of the tunnel with one hand. With the other, he tries to find a steady place for his cane, but it sinks halfway into the sand.

Nick is pushing the boat out as quickly as he can, but we're not moving fast enough. I grasp the side of the boat and dig my nails into the wet wood, and Nick, standing in the water beside me, covers my hand with his. Even in the icy rain, his touch is warm, and I slightly relax my cramping fingers.

Moments later, Scars climbs out of the tunnel and stands on the beach beside Marcos. He places his foot in the sand by Marcos's cane, and Marcos steadies his cane on Scars's shoe. For a moment, as Marcos stands there in the rain, wet and dirty and pathetic as an old, lame dog, I almost feel sorry for him. I know what it feels like to love someone and not be loved in return. *What does that do to someone after fifteen years?*

But then Marcos points at us, floating in the lake less than twenty feet away, and his eyes nearly pop out of his skull. His skin flushes a deep, angry red . . . and then he explodes, and all of his evil and ugliness comes crawling out. "Get back here!" Marcos screams, his voice creeping onto the boat and sliding under my skin.

The rain pounds the water between us, and billions of circles of water swim across the surface, blending into each other in the silver glint of the moon.

"There's nowhere to go," Marcos yells across the tiny beach.

"Away from you!" I scream back.

Marcos says something to Scars, and Scars pulls a gun out of his jacket and aims it across the beach at us. Instantly, the distance separating us from the shore seems to shrink into nothing.

Nick, his hand still covering mine, is standing beside the boat, up to his hips in water. "Let them go," Nick shouts into the rain, his words catapulting across the water and sand between us.

"Get in," I shriek.

Nick turns around to climb into the boat, but a bullet hits the water beside him. Suddenly, I know it's too late: if Nick tries to get on the boat, Scars will shoot him. *That was just a warning.* My stomach plummets as Scars lifts his gun again and points it at Nick, and the world slows to an unbearable crawl.

"Don't move!" Marcos yells.

Nick freezes. He looks back and forth between me and Marcos, only his eyes moving in the rainy night. Then his hand tightens over mine, and he turns to face the beach, putting his body between Marcos and me.

"Think carefully, Nicolas," Marcos shouts. "Don't do something you'll regret."

"Don't talk to me about regret!" Nick yells.

"Pull the boat in," Marcos yells back.

Nick squeezes my wet hand in his, and then he extends

his arms and grabs hold of the boat's stern with both hands.

"That's right, Nicolas," Marcos says. "Pull it in."

Nick looks at me, and sadness is so deeply etched in his face I could drown in it. "Follow the shoreline left," he whispers. "Around the island. The boat will be there. Look for the Santa Muerte flag."

I thrust out my other hand and grab his. It's a block of ice. "I'm not leaving without you."

"The boat," Marcos orders from the shore, pulling a gun from the pocket of his red silk jacket. "Pull it in."

"I promised I'd protect you," Nick says, pulling his arms back and spreading his fingers. Then he shoves the boat as hard as he can.

I grab for his hand, but it slips out of mine, and Mom and I float out into the dark lake. "NICK!" I scream as we float farther and farther from him. With every inch, he fades more into the wall of pounding rain. Soon I can see only Nick's red jersey, twisting like a matador's cape as he tries to run through the waist-high water. Scars's massive legs pump up and down as he sprints into the lake, toward Nick. On the beach, Marcos is hopping on one foot, desperately trying to yank his cane out of the sand and steady his gun on Nick at the same time.

As I float farther away, I see Scars's huge body breaking through the waves, rain battering his bald head as he bulls forward. Nick is running through the water, his body jerking backward with each incoming wave, but Scars is faster, and as he reaches Nick, rain runs into my eyes, briefly blinding me.

"NICK!" I scream as Scars knocks Nick into the water, his red jersey disappearing into the dark lake. Gunshots explode in the air, golden flares bursting across the night sky before fading into the gray rain. Every golden burst pauses the rain, and I can see each individual raindrop, frozen in the air on its way to earth.

"NICK!" I scream again and again, until I gag on the water filling up my mouth. The rain's coming down so hard I can barely see the beach, and only the sound of gunshots and the rain whipping the water fills my ears. I can't see Nick anymore, or hear his voice, and I have no way of knowing if he's still alive. *He has to be.*

I grab the oars and shove them into the lake. They stick in the water, so heavy I can barely hold on to them. *I won't leave him.* I steel my legs against the boat, preparing to row toward Nick. *I have to save him.*

But then I look at Mom, so helpless on the boat floor. Her skin is a layer of goose bumps in the freezing rain, and she's curled on her side, grimacing, her skinny arms holding her stomach. *I can't go back. She's depending on me.*

What do I do? Indecision rakes my muscles and mind into thin strips of raw pain. *Go back and try to rescue Nick? How do I know if he's still alive?* I look at the shore, where the rain has erased everything but a few dark spots in the field of gray. *He saved my life. And I love him.* I shiver as the icy water splashes over my legs, making the white cloth transparent. *But what about Mom? She could die out here if I don't get her help.* My head is pulling apart, my body ripping between the people I love. *What should I do?* The rain stings my skin, but inside, every part of me is tearing in two. *I can't beat Marcos and Scars, but I can save Mom. And maybe if I get to Nick's cousin fast enough, he might be able to help Nick.*

I force myself to drag the oars through the black water, propelling us away from the beach. *Follow the shoreline to the left.* My muscles are screaming as I haul my arms backward, my knuckles are cracking, and I can't tell the difference between the rain and my tears. I have to squint to see a foot in front of me, and the shore is rapidly disappearing behind the curtain of water.

I follow the shoreline toward the cove, my lower back aching every time I pull back on the oars, my calf muscles cramping from pressing my feet against the boat floor. I'm coughing and choking and snot is dripping into my mouth and I want Nick so bad I can feel it. But Mom's in the fetal position on the floor, shaking with cold, and I have to get her to someone soon. *Keep going. Just a little longer.*

My fingers are slipping off the oars, but I keep rowing left until I curve around the island. When I look back, I can't see the beach anymore. I'm scared and I'm wet and my hands are blistered from the heavy paddles, but I've got to keep going.

I'm rowing with every last bit of strength I have when I see a flag flapping in the wind. I stand up and wave my arms. "Over here!"

I hear yelling, and the boat's headlights flip on, illuminating the flag of Santa Muerte, the grim reaper in a bridal gown, dancing in the heavy rain.

"GET NICK!" I yell as the boat pulls forward, engine whining. The flag of Santa Muerte sways closer.

Tears stream down my face as I squint into the approaching lights of the rescue boat. *Nick's cousin is coming for Mom and me. We're going home.* But it feels like my home is fading away, into the dark night. As the ice-cold water splashes against my face, Isla Rosales disappears into the blackness, taking Nick with it. Like he was never there at all.

As Nick's cousin helps us onto the boat, I can only remember the last time I was in this lake, skin to skin, the ice inside me melting and floating away. I remember the stars exploding above our heads, his lips on mine, and the complete peace I felt, nestled in Nick's arms. I remember sharing our secrets by the crackling fire, and peering through the cut in his armor, into the deep hole inside of him, and how I wanted to tell him that it was his hole, not his armor, that made him strong. I remember how I'd wanted to say, "I see your soul," but I was too embarrassed. And now, as the boat pulls away, taking Nick away from me forever, I think that it was my soul I was seeing too, that night around the campfire. And maybe, as I got to know Nick, I got to know myself.

Nick's cousin wraps me in a blanket, and it's instantly soaking in the rain, but I don't feel the cold, or the way my knees are stinging or my head pounding. I just know that all those days in Mexico, I wasn't a coward. I was scared, but I didn't let it stop me. I gritted my teeth and pushed through it. And to my surprise, I wasn't helpless or weak. I was strong—stronger than I ever knew I could be.

Epilogue

WHEN I THINK ABOUT IT now, I think about all the things I could have done differently. What if I'd run faster through the tunnel, or if I'd believed Nick in the funeral home, or if I'd rowed back to shore? Mom says I'm torturing myself. She says I need to be more like the Holy Fool in the tarot deck, ready to step off the precipice into my future and leave regrets of the past behind. "Nobody knows where they're going," Mom says, "until they get there."

I think differently. I think I should have been able to see my fate from the time I got off the broken-down bus in Mexico and met the most complicated, most beautiful man in the world. I should have known that I would never end up in his arms, wrapped in seashells and pearls, but that I'd always be here, in this city of money and fame and emptiness.

When we got back to the city a month ago, the police suggested we go into the witness protection program, like the Mexican government did for Isabel, Paloma, and Abuelita, but I refuse to hide anymore. I don't want to cower behind a wall of ice that I fear will crack and drown me. I want to live without fear, because, like Isabel said, everything, even the death of one we love, is a wound that heals over time. And then you can live through anything.

Mom's proof of that. She's working her way into life again, and the doctors say she'll be back to normal soon. In the meantime, I'm spending every second by her side, helping her relearn the simplest tasks, like signing autographs and dodging the paparazzi. Teaching her the same things she once taught me.

My dad is bursting at the seams he's so happy we're back, although Mom said that may change when he finds out he's not my real father. When we first got home, he hugged me for what seemed like an hour, his tears dripping down my hair, and then he said, "I'll never ignore my little girl again." I grimaced on the outside, but I liked when he said that. I liked the sound of it: *little girl*. Like I'm still protected and trusting, safe from a world that keeps trying to crush me, but hasn't succeeded yet.

I'm not allowed to open my own fan mail anymore, but I secretly opened a letter from Mary the other day. They don't allow her to send much from prison, so they blacked out everything but the last two words: "I'm sorry." I'm learning how to forgive her, because I know now that desperation drives people to do crazy things. I should know. I'm going crazy I'm so desperate to find Nick. But the CIA claims Marcos has disappeared into thin air, taking Nick with him.

And Pierre and Sparrow, well, they begged my forgiveness, and I gave it to them. Pierre has the right to fall in love too, I guess, even if it's not with me. I'm angry with them, and I avoid them like the plague, but they did try to save my life, after all. I still find it strange that they saw Mary, the night before I got the DVD, talking to the FBI agent with the two different-colored eyes. "He warned her that he was watching her," Sparrow said. "He said he didn't have enough evidence yet to arrest her, and Mary said that he never would."

The FBI agent, it turns out, was trying to protect me. He had found out about Mary, and was trying to stop her that day in the limo. He came down to Mexico looking for me, and even followed me as far as Nick's cousin's house. But then Scars caught up with him, and he ended up dead in the woods. Pierre said that the FBI didn't do enough to protect me, but Sparrow, now always glued to Pierre's side, said that nobody thought Mary would really do what she did.

I know I should be angrier with them, and their love-tainted smiles on every magazine cover should drive me up the wall, but right now, my heart and mind are so full of Nick I have no space left to be angry. Dad said the police are looking for Nick every hour I am thinking of him, which is always. I have to believe he is still alive.

Every time I breathe, I inhale on *Find*, and exhale on *Nick*.

Find Nick.
Find Nick.
Find Nick.

I wonder what language Nick is hearing right now, if they use letters or symbols. I wonder if he can still feel my lips on his, if I'll ever see him again, and I wonder if he thinks I'm left with no one to save me, or if he knows that I don't need anyone to save me anymore. I can save myself.

Acknowledgments

BEING A TEENAGER IS AN act of courage.

If you are going through it, you know what I'm talking about. (And hang in there—it gets better!) If you've already been through it, you know too, with the help of hindsight.

That's why I wrote this book.

How is another question entirely.

The *how* is thanks to some amazing people, most of them listed below:

I will be forever grateful to Katherine Tegen, my phenomenal editor, for taking a chance on me and making this book all that it is. I couldn't have done it without you.

Thanks also to Katie Bignell, who continually smoothed the publishing path so I didn't stumble. And to the rest of the incredible Harper team, who have made my transition into publishing a joyful one: Stephanie Evans, Lauren Flower, Casey McIntyre, Amy Ryan, Joel Tippie, Martina Flor, Kathryn Silsand, Marie Claire Cebrian-Ume, and the entire Harper sales team.

Speaking of grateful, I am eternally thankful to my wise and wonderful agent, Jodi Reamer. She looked out for me every step of the way and provided me with extra courage and confidence. She is truly a magic maker. Thanks also to Alec Shane, for all of the great work you do behind the scenes.

Thanks to the SCBWI UK, particularly Sara Grant and Sara O'Connor, for shedding light on the first ten pages of this book. Your hard work gave this book the jump-start it needed, and I will always appreciate it.

Thanks also to David Ford and Brett Brubaker. You gave me the courage to move forward with this book, and your sage advice helped make this dream real.

To my spectacular writing groups, I couldn't have done this without you. Tara Dairman and Laura Resau, your friendships and writing advice are priceless. Thanks for encouraging me every step of the way. Also a huge thanks to Cindy Strandvold, Jenny Goebel, Todd Mitchell, Sarah Ryan, Carrie Visintainer, Leslie Patterson, Laura Katers, and my teacher Keith Abbott.

Thanks also to my beloved artistic Granddaddy, my Alabama family, and all of my dear friends, for helping keep my spirits up, and to Jan, for giving me a place to write in New York.

I'm sending a big thank-you to my Missouri family (Phyllis, Jimmy, Olivia, and Alexey) for welcoming me into the farm life and supporting me through this whole process. I also owe a big thank-you to my Aurora family (Mike and Ellen) for giving me a place to relax when I was most stressed. And to Helena, for being a grandmother to me, and loving me even when I was a pain in the arse.

Thanks also to Allison, Danny, Fletcher, and Madeleine for providing me with lots of joy and laughter. I love you to the moon. To Alli, my wonderful sister, who took the time to send out my first writings to publishers and accept all of the rejections for me. I am forever grateful.

I am overwhelmed with gratitude for my amazing parents, John and Vivian Sabel. They have always encouraged me to follow my dreams and taught me how to live life to the fullest. They are the most inspiring people I know. They gave me wings and believed I could fly—and I can! Thank you, thank you, thank you!

To my husband, Tyler. Without you, there would be no book. There would be no mischievous smile behind the words, no absurdly huge love pulling it along, page by page.

I don't have enough words to thank you with. Just know that all of my journeys have been roads leading to you, and if you are the destination, I am home.

And to my readers, thank you. You are a dream come true.